D0056131

a KIND of PARADISE

Amy Rebecca Tan

HARPER

An Imprint of HarperCollinsPublishers

A Kind of Paradise
Copyright © 2019 by Amy Rebecca Tan
All rights reserved. Printed in the United States of America. No part of this book may
be used or reproduced in any manner whatsoever without written permission except in
the case of brief quotations embodied in critical articles and reviews. For information
address HarperCollins Children's Books, a division of HarperCollins Publishers, 195
Broadway, New York, NY 10007.
www.harpercollinschildrens.com

Names: Tan, Amy Rebecca, author.
Title: A kind of paradise / Amy Rebecca Tan.
Description: First edition. | New York, NY : Harper, an imprint of HarperCollins
  Publishers, [2019] | Summary: Thirteen-year-old Jamie must spend her summer
  volunteering at Foxfield Public Library, but quickly grows to love the people there
  and enthusiastically joins the fight to save the library.
Identifiers: LCCN 2018034253 | ISBN 9780062795410 (hardback)
Subjects: | CYAC: Libraries—Fiction. | Interpersonal relations—Fiction. |
Community service (Punishment)—Fiction. | Single-parent families—Fiction. |
  BISAC: JUVENILE FICTION / Family / Alternative Family. | JUVENILE
  FICTION / Books & Libraries. | JUVENILE FICTION / Social Issues /
  Friendship.
Classification: LCC PZ7.1.T367 Kin 2019 | DDC [Fic]—dc23 LC record available at
  https://lccn.loc.gov/2018034253

Typography by ebb-n-flo
19 20 21 22 23 CG/LSCH   10 9 8 7 6 5 4 3 2 1
❖
First Edition

To Mike, Nina, and Jeffrey
for being my everything.
and for believing.
always

prologue

➤➤➤·⟨⟨⟨

My mom's favorite piece of advice was "Know the players. If you know who you're dealing with, you'll know
how to deal. You'll know how to play the game."

She told me if I followed that advice, I'd never get into
trouble.

Another one she liked a lot was "Know when to fold and
walk away."

Also, "Don't play cards you don't have."

She knew a lot of gambling-related sayings and loved to
pass them on to me like sacred words of wisdom from a revered
ancestor. But really she got them all from the years she spent
serving drinks to strangers at a casino in Atlantic City. Her job
was to strut around for hours in uncomfortable shoes delivering
trays of drinks to people who dropped money on the table like

it was nothing more than lint from the bottom of an old bag. She said she made decent money there, but you wouldn't find another shred of decent in a casino if you looked behind every glitzy mirror and under every polished table and chair in the whole joint.

The casino was where she met my dad, of course.

This was before she learned how important it was to know the players. This was before she knew how important it was to tuck your emotions down deep into your back pocket every now and again, just long enough to clear your head and figure out exactly who you were dealing with. This was way before she had me, before she left my dad, before she moved the two of us to Foxfield, the small sidewalk town in central Pennsylvania that's the only home I've ever known, to be closer to my aunt Julie. We moved into a tiny brick house with two cracked cement steps leading to the front door and identical square windows on either side, like two perfect dimples. She burned her high-heeled casino shoes and bought white clogs and took a job behind the reception desk at a dental office.

That move happened before I turned two, and I hadn't seen my dad since. I have no memory of him at all.

What my mom also needed to tell me, but never did, was *Know yourself.* If she had taught me that, maybe I would have stopped myself. Maybe I would have been smarter.

Maybe I would have heard the voice in my head reminding me who I was that afternoon back in May: straight-A seventh grader, aspiring artist and member of the Art Club, kindergarten reading buddy, thoughtful daughter and niece.

Maybe I would have heard the voice in my head reminding me who I wasn't: cheater, liar, thief.

Maybe then I would have left the book where I found it.

Or maybe I would have turned it in to the principal.

Maybe I wouldn't have been humiliated in front of the entire middle school population.

And maybe I wouldn't be spending my summer "paying my dues" as a volunteer at the Foxfield Public Library.

Maybe.

JUNE

Black Hat Guy

->>>·<<<-

The guy in the black hat pushed through the front door like a gust of angry wind, grunting under his breath as he went. He was hunched over himself the way he always was, his shoulders curved, his eyes pinned to the ground. He stormed past the circulation desk without looking up, past the row of public computer stations and the entire wall of New Fiction, his head shaking side to side the whole way. I was new at the library—it was Monday of my second week—but Black Hat Guy moved through the space like it was his own living room. It was clear he had been coming here for a while.

I heard the words *tyrant* and *coffee shop* and *sludge* as I kept my eyes down and nested the *Daily News* sections back inside themselves. The only coffee shop in town was the Bean Pot. It had free Wi-Fi and served really thick hot chocolate with free whipped cream topping, which made it a popular after-school hangout. I never went there. I had no relationship with the word *popular* at all, unless you put the words *not even remotely* in front of it.

From the way Black Hat Guy was ranting under his breath, it sounded like the Bean Pot wasn't a great match for him either. At least he didn't have to worry about tyrants or sludge at the library. He could sit here all day if he wanted to.

I knew it was between 4:00 and 4:12 p.m. without even looking at the clock, because that's when Black Hat Guy came to the library every day.

Every. Day.

I also figured Black Hat Guy must have some kind of medical condition that left him immune to outdoor temperatures, because it was a sweaty eighty-eight-degree day, but you'd never know it from the black sweatshirt, jeans, and winter knit hat he was wearing. And had worn every day of the summer so far.

Every. Day.

I tucked the Sports section inside the Arts section, even though it was supposed to go the other way around. It was pretty much the only power I had as the library's one volunteer— to order the newspaper sections to my liking, or to choose which books to face out on a shelf. Art trumped sports, and a biography of my favorite painter, Georgia O'Keeffe, trumped any book on boxing champions and always would.

Black Hat Guy huffed his way over to the chair by the window.

He always went to the same chair.

Always.

It was the one upholstered in an ivory-colored fabric, with literary quotes printed in black cursive all over it. At least, I thought they were all literary. Some I knew for sure, like *To be or not to be* and *Call me Ishmael* and *Quoth the Raven "Nevermore."* Pretty much everyone knew those even if they didn't know who wrote them or what books they were from. Then there were other quotes that sounded familiar, but I wasn't sure if they were just familiar because I had read them on the chair a dozen times already or because I actually knew them from life, like *Tread softly because you tread on my dreams* and *What is essential is invisible to the eye.* There were others still that could have been completely made up, for all I knew, like *Time changes everything except something within us which is always surprised by change.*

That's a famous quote? Really?

Famous for making zero sense, maybe.

Black Hat Guy pulled a charger from his pocket and plugged one end into an outlet under the window, the plate loose and jiggling side to side as he pushed the plug in. Then he sank into his chair, pulled his hat lower onto his brow, retracted his head into his sweatshirt collar, which made him look like a grumpy old turtle, and promptly went to sleep.

It was amazing. Never in a million years could I walk into a public place in a foul mood, have a seat, and completely zonk out to Snoozeville in a matter of two minutes flat, but Black Hat Guy could. And did.

At least he didn't snore.

Beverly

➤➤➤·⫷⫷⫷

"I clicked *print*. I CLICKED IT ALREADY!" a patron on computer number four yelled at the screen in front of him.

Several patrons lifted their heads at the outburst, including a man sitting just two computers down from the yeller, but not one of them offered to help. The man at computer four was red in the face and sweating and looked about as approachable as a rabid raccoon.

Beverly emerged from her cramped library director's office in the back of the building. Even if the swish of her slacks didn't announce her arrival ahead of her, you could see her coming from clear across the building because of her red hair, a deep red so fiery bright it was impossible to miss. She probably had to buy every packet of red hair dye at the pharmacy and mix them all together to get a shade that red. But hair color was the only flashy thing about Beverly. She didn't wear a drop of makeup, her nails were never painted, and she didn't put on earrings or even a watch. She wore no jewelry at all aside from a gold necklace around her neck, so neatly tucked inside her shirt that it took me a whole week before I even realized it was there.

"Good afternoon, sir. Is this computer acting up on you?" Beverly ran her hands down the sides of her pants, as if to shush them, and clasped her hands together. "Maybe I can help."

The man glared at the computer screen through glasses so smudged it was a wonder he could see through them at all.

"It won't print my ticket! I clicked it a thousand times," he sputtered, hands up in total frustration.

I tried not to laugh at the thought of a thousand copies of whatever ticket he was trying to print flying out of the printer as soon as Beverly fixed it. But Beverly would fix that, too. Beverly could fix everything—the printer, the computer server, the Xerox copier, even the security system. She had master technician skills to go with her master librarian skills.

"Let's see if we can't persuade it to cooperate. If I may," Beverly said, leaning over him toward the keyboard.

It took her less than fifteen seconds to get the ticket to print.

The yeller thanked her and Beverly assured him it was no trouble at all. She didn't even make it three steps toward her office, though, before another patron stopped her for help.

"Excuse me, ma'am," a woman in perfectly coordinated head-to-toe workout gear called to Beverly.

I noticed on my first day that people in the library called Beverly *ma'am*. They called me *miss*, if they called me at all.

"Yes, how may I help you?" Beverly asked, rubbing her hands down the sides of her pants again and then clasping them in front of her as she smiled at the woman. She did that routine with her hands all the time, like a nervous twitch. I noticed that my first day here, too.

"I've been waiting for a book forever. I'm on the hold list and it was supposed to be back a long time ago." She put her hands on her hips and huffed. "It's not right that someone can keep a book for that long. These books are public property!"

"I'm so sorry you've been waiting," Beverly apologized right away. "If you would please follow me to a computer, I can look up the title and see what's going on."

Beverly led her to a circulation computer, typed in the title, and nodded as she clicked and read the screen. She reported back, "Yes, I see it is quite overdue. I'll put in an order for a copy from another library while I follow up with the person who has it out. That way I can assure you get the book in a timely manner. How does that sound?" She smiled and nodded again.

It wasn't policy to borrow books from other libraries when we owned our own copy—Beverly explained that to me last week—but I guess she thought this angry woman was worth bending a rule for.

"If that's all we can do, fine," the workout lady answered, not even trying to hide her irritation.

Maybe she needed a good workout to calm her down. It was just a book, after all.

"I think this will solve our problem," Beverly assured her, nodding some more. "I'm so sorry for the inconvenience. You'll be notified as soon as it arrives."

The woman managed a half smile as she turned on her heel and sauntered out without saying thank you. Beverly didn't seem the least bit bothered by it, though. It was like my mom said: Beverly knew the players. She knew who she was dealing with, so she knew how to deal. Maybe Beverly had worked in casinos before she worked in libraries and that was where she got so good at it.

I would much rather spend my summer in a loud, dark casino, where I could hide behind tall barstools and fat slot machines, than in this old, musty, creaky library. But I'm pretty sure they don't let thirteen-year-old middle-school mess-ups volunteer at casinos.

Though I wasn't exactly volunteering at the library, either.

I was *forced* to work here. ("Try not to think of it as a punishment, Jamie," Principal Shupe advised. "But our Honor Code is the backbone of the middle school. Of course there are consequences for violating it." She leaned back in her fancy principal chair a bit and said, more gently, "I'm just sorry it's you who has to face those consequences." And she did look sorry, for about half a second, and then that drop of empathy evaporated faster than a raindrop on hot summer pavement. She launched into an explanation of my community service assignment and told me that I would have to hand in a list detailing what I learned from the experience at the end. *And* I had to write an apology letter to Trey.)

Mrs. Shupe could call it a *consequence* all she wanted, but trust me: if your school and your mom were making you spend fifteen hours a week, *every week*, of your summer vacation working for free, it's a punishment.

The two-week sleepaway art camp I'd hoped to go to this summer—gone. A week at the beach with Aunt Julie—gone. A road trip to New Hampshire with my best friend Vic's parents to visit her at camp—don't even think about it. And it wasn't like I could hang out at the local pool between my library hours—there would be people there, *middle school* people— and those were the last people on earth I wanted to see. My summer was going to be a sad combination of time at the library and time alone in my tiny backyard, drawing and reading and staring at a lonely blue sky.

So on top of all the knots already twisting around in my stomach about what the entire middle school population was saying about me behind my back, I also had to worry about getting along with the library staff. Either Beverly had the best poker face in the whole entire world or she was a complete saint, because she didn't seem the least bit wary about having some kid assigned to community service at her library.

Beverly never asked me what I had done or why. She just acted like I was another member of her cherished library staff.

I watched her pick up a piece of scrap paper from the worn tile floor, drop it in a recycling bin, then take a quick head count of patrons in the reading room before walking over to check on me.

"Everything all right here, Jamie?" Beverly asked me.

"Yeah," I answered, then corrected myself. "Yes."

"The newspapers look great," she said.

"Thank you. I just finished them," I said, smiling at her.

Her eyes scanned the room and came to a stop on Black Hat Guy, still slumped asleep in the quotes chair, the rise and fall of his chest barely noticeable under his thick sweatshirt. The wire to the wall outlet was stretched taut, like a guitar string about to snap.

She nodded at his sleeping body, then turned and smiled at me and said, "Yes, well, okay," which I translated in my head to mean, *Yes, we are here to serve the public in any way we can.* I smiled back again, and then I just looked down at my sneakers and acted like I needed to fix my laces in order to escape the nodding-smiling loop. Beverly walked to the front desk to check in with Sonia.

That was Beverly—supersmart and patient and genuine, with just a touch of awkward. But so what? What was so bad about awkward? Awkward was honest. Awkward was real.

And after getting busted for cheating, after having my private crush outed to *everyone*, I had a pretty solid relationship with awkward.

Wally

>>>·<<<

"Good morning to you, and a good morning it is," Wally half sang, half stated his greeting as he pushed through the library door the next morning.

"Hello there, miss," he said to me as he approached the circulation desk to return his items. "It's nice to see you again. Jamie, is it?"

"Yes, that's right. It's nice to see you, too," I answered, smiling politely at him. "And you're Wally, right?" I asked, even though I was sure. I had heard a lot about Wally from Sonia and Lenny, the other two permanent staff members besides Beverly. Wally was a Tuesday morning regular at the library and had been for years. He was a total movie fanatic, except he used the word *flick* instead of *movie*. He watched everything: classics, westerns, action, comedy, drama, even foreign. And he always checked out five movies at a time. Every Tuesday morning.

"Good memory!" Wally said, his eyes opening a little wider in surprise. "That's the first step to excellent customer service. Very well done."

I smiled at the compliment and blushed a little. "Thanks."

"I'll be seeing you every week now, I guess," Wally said.

"I'll be here for the summer."

"Well then, you'll be seeing me!"

He slid his five movies into the return bin on the counter and told me, "Really good flicks I watched this week. Really good. You might like 'em."

"Okay, thanks. I'll take a look."

"*War Games*—it's a classic. You seen it?" Wally asked.

I shook my head no.

"My kids' favorite when they were growing up. One of my wife's, too, God rest her soul." Wally put his hand over his heart when he said that.

I didn't know what to say, because he'd basically just told me, without saying it word for word, that his wife was dead. I didn't know if it just happened recently or if she'd been gone for a long time, but if he was watching a favorite family movie, he must miss her.

"So I should watch it?" I asked, trying to steer us away from death and back toward movies—flicks—instead.

"Highly recommend it!" Wally said, removing his large, pale hand from his chest and giving me a thumbs-up sign with it. "All this smart kid wants to do is hack computers to find new video games to play, but a few wrong clicks and he ends up starting a real global war."

"Whoa!" I let out a gasp-shout combo, a little too loud for a library.

Wally chuckled at my response. "Oh, it's a great one." Then he grinned with his whole face, the wrinkles around his eyes scrunching, and explained, "Of course, my kids were already crazy for video games when that flick came out, so that was why. They spent probably half their childhood sitting on the basement floor playing Atari."

Atari.

That was my mom's childhood favorite, too. My mom worshiped her Atari system and all the games she had collected to play on it. She still hadn't forgiven her own mother for chucking them when she moved out.

"She was mad at me for choosing a college so far away," my mom explained. "It was one of the meanest things she ever did to me."

"That's cold," I agreed.

"My most sacred childhood possession." My mom shuddered.

"I'm glad I don't have to worry about that," I said.

My mom looked up from the sink, where she was scrubbing a pot. "What do you mean?"

"I mean you hated how that felt, when your mom trashed your toy—"

"Do *not* call it a toy!" My mom pointed her soapy sponge at me threateningly.

"I mean, when your mom trashed your 'most sacred childhood possession,'" I corrected myself, rolling my eyes, "so I know you'd never do that to me. When I go to college."

"Yeah, don't be so sure about that," she told me, returning to her pot scrubbing.

"What?"

"I'm just saying, I hear weird things happen to you when your kids move out." She shook her head.

"Like, you get super mean?" I asked.

"No." She let the pot fill halfway with soapy water to soak. "Well, maybe."

"Fantastic," I said, rolling my eyes again.

"My mother still had your aunt Julie at home with her when I left. You're my only kid, so it will probably be extra bad for me when you leave."

"Jeez, Mom!"

"At least you know in advance," she told me, as if this was all completely out of her hands. "Take your special stuff with you. Or hide it. Really, *really* well."

"Or just, like, go to college two miles from here," I said, staring her down.

"Yes, two miles. I'll give you up to ten, maybe, before my mean meter ticks on. Eleven, tops."

"Gee, Mom. You're the best."

"I try."

"It's a good thing I don't have my own Atari to lose."

"Greatest. Games. Ever." And then she went back to scrubbing, humming under her breath.

Vic and I searched online for Atari commercials one day after we came home from school to find my mom belting the jingle from the bathroom, her voice echoing off the tile walls. She kept singing it over and over again: *"Have you played Atari today?"*

Vic and I cracked up watching the old commercials—the grainy footage, the terrible animation, the dated clothes and haircuts on the actors. It was hard to believe that games like *Asteroids* and *Space Invaders* could ever have been popular. They looked so amateur and basic to us.

"Are you disrespecting my childhood passion?" my mom called from the bathroom when our giggles went on for too long.

"No, never, Ms. Bunn," Vic answered immediately, then covered her mouth and laughed so hard she fell off her chair.

"Rome wasn't built in a day, kiddos," my mom lectured over the sound of a bristle brush scrubbing back and forth. "Those games were revolutionary when they came out."

Vic and I raised our eyebrows at each other, and Vic whispered, "What's Rome got to do with it?"

Then we cracked up even more, but quietly.

"You do realize those kids in the commercial are seventy years old now," Vic informed me once she caught her breath.

"Not seventy," I answered, calculating in my head. "More like midforties."

"Whatever, math geek," she said, hitting the replay button so we could watch it one more time.

I heard my mom singing the last line of the ad again. *"Have you played Atari today?"*

I liked hearing the song in my mom's voice more than the original recorded version. She sang it with heart—you could actually hear how special her Atari memories were in the rise and fall of her breath as she sang. It was way better than the song spewing from the laptop speaker.

"Okay, Wally," I said, picking up the *War Games* DVD and looking at the pictures on the back of the case. "Maybe I'll watch it."

"All righty." Wally gave me another thumbs-up. "You won't

be disappointed." And then he made his face all serious and, in a bad robotic voice recited, "Shall. We. Play. A. Game?" Then he gripped the circulation counter between us and laughed.

"Umm," I stalled. "I'm . . . guessing that's from the movie?" I half said, half asked.

"You guessed right!" Wally laughed again. Then he had to stop laughing to cough. His cough was loud and guttural and phlegmy and made me want to back up about a thousand steps. He was good about it, though, and covered his mouth with the arm that wasn't holding on to the counter, and he turned his head away from me. Then he cleared his throat, righted himself, turned back to face me, and laughed again. "Do excuse me," he said.

"You are excused," I said.

"All right then, time to look for five new ones. Gotta stick to my routine. Tuesday's my day." He grinned at me, a super-wide, happy grin. His teeth were crooked and gray and many were missing, but he smiled like he didn't know it, or knew it but didn't care about hiding it.

I liked that. His mouth looked awful, but it didn't stop him from smiling. He was cheerful and polite and responsible— his movies were never late—and that mattered to him a whole lot more than how he looked. I wished I could get Wally to walk through the middle school halls and spread some of that around.

"I'll do my looking now," Wally told me as he motioned toward his DVD wall. "Thanks a lot, dear."

"Sure," I answered, even though I hadn't done anything for him to thank me for.

"Oh, almost forgot my flower," Wally said. He pulled a single-stem carnation out of a ratty plastic grocery bag. The flower was yellow this week.

Wally took last Tuesday's wilted pink flower out of the squat glass jar pretending to be a vase at the end of the circulation desk and tossed it into his bag. Then he carefully slid the new flower into the jar, turned it to his liking, and said, "There she is."

"Very pretty," I told him, even though it was kind of a sad-looking flower.

Wally brought a flower with him on each of his Tuesday visits. It was very cool of Beverly to allow it, since you'd think she wouldn't want an open container of water around the books and computers.

Wally wobbled around the reference desk, coughing and leaning on furniture on either side as he went, to get to his movie wall and begin his weekly search.

Sonia

➤➤➤·◄◄◄

Sonia put down her coffee cup where she always kept it, right above the money drawer, and grabbed a book with a white slip sticking out of it from the counter. "Watch the desk for me a minute, okay, Jamie?"

She swung herself out from behind the circulation desk.

"Sonia, I can't—" I started, but her lightning-fast steps got her to the door and outside before I could finish my sentence. I stepped into her spot behind the desk and hoped no one came over for help. I didn't know the first thing about how to use the circulation computers.

I stood on one foot behind the desk, then shifted my weight to the other foot. I started to pick at my fingernail but quickly stopped when I remembered I wasn't alone in my bedroom at home where no one could see me.

Alone in my bedroom at home was where I wanted to be, where I wanted to spend every second of my life since that horrific Wednesday in May. Although, if I were being truly honest, I would admit that my first choice would have been to dig a deep hole and climb in so I could hide from all life-forms for a good fifteen years. Second choice would have been to run away to Australia, like that kid Alexander from the book about the terrible, horrible, no good, very bad day.

Hibernating in my bedroom at home was my third choice. And even that turned out to be a very bad option those first few days after it all blew up and Mrs. Shupe called my mom into the school for a meeting. A meeting that the vice principal, my homeroom teacher, and the guidance counselor also attended. My mom came home from that meeting so distraught she could barely even look at me. And when she finally did look at me, her face was a mask of confusion, like she didn't recognize me at all, like she wanted to know who in God's name was that stranger in her living room who looked just like her daughter.

A lump the size of my fist swelled in my throat when she looked at me like that.

I apologized and told her I knew what I did was beyond dumb but that I couldn't take it, her being so mad at me. She only shook her head.

"I'm not mad, Jamie." Her voice was the saddest whisper in

the world. "I'm disappointed."

Her words made me want to crumple into the smallest ball possible and disappear.

"You had a chance to fold, Jamie. You had a chance to walk away. Why didn't you?" she asked, her eyes pleading, desperate to understand.

I opened my mouth to answer but nothing came out.

"I didn't know it was possible to feel this disappointed," she said again, which felt exactly like a knife twisting in a raw, gaping wound.

And I knew it was true, her disappointment, because she called my aunt Julie then and they went out to dinner without me.

They had never gone out to dinner without me before. Ever.

Restaurants were *our* thing—as in all three of us.

Aunt Julie loved to say, "We might live in small Podunk towns, but we travel the globe through our palates!"

And we really did. Aunt Julie thought nothing of a forty-five-minute drive just to try a new restaurant serving cuisine from another part of the world. We had tried Japanese, Moroccan, Indian, French, and even Ethiopian, where we ate with our hands and used a kind of soft flatbread to scoop up our food instead of forks. But Chinese remained our all-time favorite, which was fortunate because it was only a ten-minute car ride away.

Aunt Julie was my mom's younger sister. She wasn't married and she didn't have kids, unless you counted all the animals she took in and provided for. *She* certainly considered them family. At the current moment, she had three dogs, two cats, and a bunny. She had worked at the same casino as my mom years back and was also a big proponent of *knowing the players*, which led her straight to a faithful love of animals.

"Nothing and no one is more honest than an animal." Aunt Julie believed this to her core. "You look at an animal and it's clear as crystal—all their intentions right there on their face where you can see them. No games. No tricks."

"Your dogs know tons of tricks," I countered.

"Those are tricks I taught them, for stimulation. Dogs have brains and need to use them. But they'll never use them to hurt you. Not ever."

It was true that none of her animals had ever hurt her, not the way I had just hurt my mom.

So when they walked in the door together two hours later, the smell that came with them told me they'd been to Jade Noodle Shop, which stung like crazy. Jade Noodle Shop was our absolute number one favorite place. The smell of smoky green tea and candied sweet duck sauce wafted off their coats.

Aunt Julie's hair, when she leaned in to say good night to me, smelled so strong of stir-fry it might as well have been a salon product she blow-dried into her hair.

When my mom wasn't looking, Aunt Julie whispered to me, "Give her time. You know how much she loves you."

The truth in Julie's words somehow made me feel both better and worse at the same time, and the tears rushed to my eyes again.

It had gotten better since then, thank God, with my mom.

"Everyone plays cards they don't have at some point—that's how they learn, from losing big," she said to me, about a week after the meeting with Mrs. Shupe. "Let this be the one bad hand you played." She said it like an order but then hugged me to soften it.

And it was like we understood each other on a whole new level after that. But I still wanted to hide from the rest of the world.

The library door opened like a gift and Sonia breezed in. Her face was flushed from the heat and she had a smudge of pink on one cheek, right above her giant smile.

"I love making people happy," Sonia told me, then gave me a light hip check to bop me out of her spot. "Did I miss anything?"

"No, no one came up," I answered, relieved that it was true. "You have something on your cheek, though."

"Oh, yes, that's my kiss. She always gives me a kiss."

"Who?"

"Sylvia Allen," Sonia said, as if she were speaking of a famous celebrity.

"Who's Sylvia Allen?"

"Sylvia Allen is a patron, and she's NINETY-SIX!" Sonia's eyes went wide. "Ninety-six years old and still driving and reading and knitting. She's my role model." Sonia's entire face lit up as she smiled. "It's good to have a role model. Believe me. It's like a compass."

"A compass?" I repeated.

"Someone to look to, to point you in the right direction."

"Oh."

"Everyone should have one," she said.

"I don't have one," I admitted. "Who should my role model be?"

Sonia squinted in thought for a moment, then announced, "Me, mami!" She bounced on her toes and let out a laugh so full she spilled her coffee. "*I* am solid role model material. By the end of the summer, you'll see." She giggled as she wiped up her spill.

I just stared at her.

Sonia smacked my shoulder as if she could push fun into me. "So serious, Jamie. We'll work on that."

She was right. I couldn't even remember the last time I had laughed hard enough to spill something. How long had it been? Weeks?

I changed the subject. "So Sylvia's still driving at ninety-six?"

"And no accidents. She's amazing! But it's hard for her to get out of the car and walk our steps, so she calls on the phone for the book she wants and I run it out to her when she pulls up."

"That's really nice of you," I admit.

"Well, don't spread the word, because I only do it for Sylvia." Sonia took a sip of her coffee. "Hmm, that went cold fast."

"You need one of those mugs with a lid, to keep the heat in," I suggested. "My mom has one."

"No, I'm fine. I'll drink my coffee at any temperature." She took another sip to illustrate her point, then added, "But see, I'd only let my coffee go cold for my role model. I'm not doing curbside for any lazy Joe who complains about rain or cold and not wanting to get out of their car. Just Sylvia. Because she's my compass."

Lenny

>>>·<<<

"Come feast your eyes on this, Jamie," Lenny called out to me from the reading room.

I trudged over with a stack of brand-new magazines and found Lenny holding open the latest *Foxfield Biweekly Newsletter*. The newsletter came out every two weeks and covered every bit of local news that could be mustered up. Foxfield was a small town, so it was a thin paper, and you knew it was an especially dry news period when the same advertisement was printed on more than one page, just to fill up space.

"Lookee here," Lenny said, holding the page lower where I could see it. Lenny had pale skin, broad shoulders, and long, graying brown hair he wore pulled back in a ponytail. And he was so tall, if he hadn't moved the paper down it would've been miles above my head. "Whaddya think of that?"

I looked at the page and read the advertisement he was pointing to: *Giant Painting Co., Lenny Bradford—free estimates, flexible scheduling, personal care, no job too big or small.* And there was a phone number printed underneath.

"Is that you?" I asked. I didn't know Lenny's last name.

"Yours truly," he answered, and bowed at the waist like he was meeting royalty. "My first print ad. I've been getting work through word of mouth, but I wanted to see if this would bring in more jobs."

"Well, I would hire you," I told him. "I like the 'Giant' part."

"Yeah, well, I figure that's my hook. There are a lot of painters out there, but how many of them are as huge as me?"

Lenny had to duck every time he went down the stairs to the staff kitchen and supply room, and his sleeves almost never reached all the way down to his wrists. He said he'd been dealing with that since the ninth grade, so he was used to it by now.

"I mean, I can reach ceilings without a ladder most of the time," he bragged. "It's a perk for painting." Then he looked up at the ceiling above us in the reading room. It was eighteen feet away, with original scalloped woodwork that was ornate and beautiful and something you would only find in a historic building. Of course, the woodwork was also stained and chipped. It definitely could've used some Lenny painting.

He craned his neck back even more to get a wider view of the ceiling design. "Most of the time I can reach," he said again, more quietly.

Lenny worked half as many hours at the library as Sonia did. He was a part-time librarian and a part-time house painter and was constantly running back and forth between the two jobs. He always changed out of his painting clothes before he came to the library, and he scrubbed his hands clean, but he wore the same shoes. His shoes were massive and impossible to miss. Thick drips and splotches of different-colored paint dotted the toe area and laces and soles and were a dead giveaway of his other job.

"Are you working on a house now?" I asked him as I started slipping the latest magazine issues into their plastic covers.

"Starting a new job today, actually. Painting a screened-in porch for someone who knew my dad back in the day. You know, my dad grew up in Foxfield," Lenny said with a certain pride.

"But you didn't?"

"Nah, I was born and raised in New Hampshire. I ended up here by, well, jeez, how *did* I end up here?" He cupped his hand around his chin and thought. "Lots of moves over the last twenty years, I guess, and I just kept going south, and south, then west." He dropped his hand from his face and shrugged. "Anyway, I've been here for years now. It's a good place to be. I'm staying put."

And then he switched into an overly animated voice to say, "Did I mention I have a business here?" He opened the newsletter again and put on a small show, gesturing at the *Giant Painting Co.* advertisement, displaying it in front of him at all angles like someone on an infomercial. But he couldn't hold a straight face and broke into laughter as he tried to get out the words, "Customer service representatives standing by now."

I had to laugh, too. He was way too old—at least in his forties—and way too large to be acting the way he was, which was like a total goofball.

"All righty then, back to work," he said after finishing his performance and rolling the *Biweekly* into a small tube to shove in his back pocket. "There's some oat bran granola bars down in the kitchen if you're hungry. They're a lot better than the last ones," he said as he walked back to the circulation desk to help patrons.

Lenny loved to invent his own recipes and baked constantly, bringing all his creations to the library for us to try. But Lenny's baked goods looked and tasted unlike any other baked goods I had seen before in my life. So far, in just the week I'd been trying them, they were hit-or-miss, a pretty even fifty-fifty split.

I finished with the magazines and straightened the stack of new *Biweekly* newspapers. Then I flipped one open to take another look at Lenny's ad. I thought of ways I would draw a decorative border around the edges, or a small design in just one corner, maybe, to spruce it up a bit if I were Lenny. I thought of the set of archival-quality felt-tip markers my mom had just given me for my thirteenth birthday. They would be perfect for this.

I closed the newsletter and my eyes landed on a front-page headline: *New Mayor Addresses Spending Cuts.* And in smaller print beneath it: *Sanitation, Police Department, Library, Fireworks.*

I looked around me, at the age-warped wooden window sashes, the threadbare carpet in one room and the pocked floor tile in another. Paint was peeling off the baseboard molding, and the shelving and desk furniture looked older than dirt. I didn't see how it would be possible to cut even a handful of nickels from the library funding—the place was already falling apart.

Of course, if it fell apart entirely, like, tomorrow, I wouldn't have to volunteer here anymore and I'd get my summer back.

One could hope.

Black Hat Guy

$\rightarrow\!\!\rangle\!\!\rangle\cdot\langle\!\langle\!\leftarrow$

The next day Black Hat Guy came into the library, walking even faster than usual, and made a beeline right for his chair. He plugged his charger in immediately, sat down, and began to type furiously on his phone. His hat was pulled low, so with his head tilted down the way it was, it looked like he didn't have any eyes. He looked like a Muppet. (*The Muppet Show* was another favorite from my mom's childhood. It was a half-hour evening show with puppetlike characters that was very funny, a little weird, and definitely not on regular TV anymore.)

His backpack sat on the floor by his feet. It was overstuffed with a grocery bag, a folded-up newspaper, and a used coffee cup sticking out of the top. I had been headed over to dust the shelves behind his chair before he came in, but decided to wait now that he was there, busy with his phone, the wire attaching him to the wall like an anchor.

I looked at the clock: 4:03.

On schedule, as usual.

It had to be almost ninety degrees outside, but he still had that winter hat on, the heavy jeans, and that thick sweatshirt. And he wasn't even sweating. It was pretty impressive, actually.

Even though Black Hat Guy was a daily visitor to the library, I'd never seen him check anything out. He seemed to use the library only for Wi-Fi, charging power, and the bathrooms. Sometimes he read the newspaper, but most of his reading was done on his phone.

One of the quotes Black Hat Guy sat on every day when he came in was *Not all those who wander are lost*. This seemed fitting for Black Hat Guy. He looked like he might be a wanderer, like someone who lived off what he could carry on his back, forging his own way. Except Black Hat Guy didn't look like a happy wanderer. He looked agitated, and confused, and very alone. He rarely spoke to anyone, never smiled, and hardly ever even looked up. It seemed like a special talent, actually, the way he moved around quickly and carefully while facing the ground. I knew I wouldn't be able to do it.

And then I looked at him in his chair again and saw that

his body blocked portions of quotes, so the beginning of one quote lined up with the ending of another. When I read straight across from his left shoulder to his right, skipping over all the words covered by his body, it said, *Call me . . . lost.*

Trina

>>>·<<<

Trina's voice was a mixture of Disney-level sweetness and barbed wire. It soared over the tinkly jingle sound the bells made when the front door opened.

"OMG, air-conditioning! Thank God!"

Trina and her two best friends entered the library the same way they entered the school cafeteria or the gym on Dance Fridays. It never occurred to them that everyone else in the world might *not* be interested in the thoughts they were having at that moment. And they didn't seem to have a clue about libraries being quiet places, either. Several patrons looked up at the sound of their chatter. Not Black Hat Guy. He was asleep and didn't budge.

"It feels sooo good in here," said Izzy, Trina's shadow.

My reflexes kicked in like a racehorse at the starting

gate—all I wanted to do was run away, fast and far, but my knees had a different idea and turned to jelly. My gut felt loose, and a rash of heat bloomed on my cheeks.

I wanted to disappear.

Today was Wednesday, June 28.

It had been five weeks.

It had been thirty-five mornings of waking up with the taste of regret and shame on my tongue. Wednesday, May 24, was the day I was called to the principal's office, the day the entire school was first shocked and then entertained by the fact that it was me, quiet, studious Jamie Bunn, who was in serious trouble. I had had thirty-five days so far to recover, but all it took was the sight of Trina for it all to come rushing back like a horrific recurring nightmare. I felt it all again—the dizziness walking down the school hallways, the nausea sitting in classes, the public humiliation following me every step I took for the last few weeks of school.

"Oh my gosh, it smells so booky," Trina said, sending her friends into an eruption of giggles.

That was Trina. Trina of the perfectly French-braided blond hair. Trina of the newest, most fashionable clothes no matter the season. Trina: posse leader, hair flipper, whiter-than-white-teeth smiler, decent track runner, and teacher kisser-upper. But Trina was not a reader. What was she doing here?

Did she come just to rub my punishment in my face?

Seeing Trina and her friends made me yearn for Vic. I missed Vic every summer when she disappeared to sleepaway camp for eight weeks, but I missed her more than ever now. I *needed* her now. Vic wasn't just my best friend—she was my only friend.

"You only need one friend to watch your poker chips when you run to the ladies' room," my mom loved to say. "One friend you can trust is better than a whole gaggle you can't."

My mom loved Vic and always had, ever since we met back in kindergarten. Vic was fun and funny and smart and loyal. My mom also said Vic was too *emotionally astute* for the average kid, and so was I, and that was why we were such a perfect match. She said that before she learned I wasn't quite as *astute* as she gave me credit for, though.

"Do they even have cookbooks in a library? They're not, like, regular books," Trina announced to her friends.

"Let's just ask someone," Amanda said.

I tiptoed backward to bury myself deeper in the 800 stacks and crouched down so I could see them but they couldn't see me. In front of my face was a row of books with the call number 811. Poetry. I was trying to become invisible against a wall of poetry. Some talented writer somewhere could probably get a good poem out of that.

I heard Sonia return to the circulation desk just then. She had been refilling her coffee cup in the staff kitchen downstairs.

"Do you girls need help with something?" she asked in her welcoming voice.

"Yes, please. We need a cookbook," Amanda started.

"But we don't know if you have cookbooks here the way a bookstore would, because libraries are different," Izzy explained.

"We're having a party and we need to make the food," Trina added, making full eye contact, her voice sweet like syrup, the overpriced kind in the really fancy bottle.

"Libraries do carry cookbooks. We have a comprehensive collection, in fact. They're in the 641 section, back and to the right." Sonia pointed them toward the back of the library.

To the room I was in.

In a small library like ours, 641 and 811 are not so far away from each other. I was trapped.

Trina led her girls around the circ desk toward the nonfiction room, staring in awe at the shelves of periodicals, movies, and books as if she were in a museum of lost artifacts. Her mouth hung open as she took it all in. When her room scan landed on Black Hat Guy, she stopped in her tracks. He was fast asleep in his chair, his mouth open, the white wire stretched from his sweatshirt pocket to the wall outlet like an IV. Trina

44

leaned in to her girls and whispered.

Then laughter. All three of them. That hand-over-the-mouth gesture of trying to look like you're trying not to laugh.

Black Hat Guy didn't flinch. But patrons around him did. They knew who the joke was about.

Sonia turned from her station at the noise.

Before she could say anything, Trina grabbed Izzy by the elbow and steered her in front, pushing her toward the 600s. They moved quickly then, in a cluster, like single cells clumped together in a glob, which we just learned about in science a few months ago. And then they were only two aisles away.

"Oh my God. Here they are!" Izzy said, all surprise and wonder *still* that a library had cookbooks. If Vic were here, we'd be rolling our eyes at each other.

"Look how many," Trina said.

"Well, let's just start," Amanda urged. "I have to be home by five to babysit."

"Oh my God, all you do is babysit," Izzy complained.

"Yeah, and I get paid, so it's awesome," Amanda defended herself.

"So let's just each pull a bunch out and flip through them until we find what we want." Trina's direction.

"Okay," Amanda agreed.

"But then how do we put them all back? Aren't they, like,

45

in order?" Izzy wanted to know.

"Of course they're in order." Trina had quickly assumed the position of library expert for her group. "But they have people for that."

"Oh," Izzy said. "Okay then, I want all these." And I heard at least six different *zip-slip* sounds of a snugly shelved book being pulled out of the stacks.

"Also, I even know who one of those *people* is," Trina offered.

I could see the evil sneer on her face.

"Who?" Izzy asked.

"You know *who*," Amanda reminded her.

"Who?" Izzy demanded, entirely clueless.

"My brother's secret admirer, that's who," Trina answered.

"But it's not a secret anymore," Amanda added.

My chest tightened.

"Oh my God! *Her.* I totally forgot!" Izzy admitted, then laughed. "I forgot she has to work it off here."

I could picture Izzy's mean smile, even though I couldn't see her face from where I was hiding. I'd seen it before.

"Yup." Trina's voice was all gossip and delight. "So take out as many books as you want. I bet she's the one who'll have to put them all back, anyway."

Then laughter.

The same laughter they shared over Black Hat Guy, except now it was about me.

It occurred to me then why Black Hat Guy might keep his eyes on the ground all the time. Maybe he did it so he wouldn't have to see any of the bad things around him. Maybe he did it so he wouldn't have to face anything mean or ugly coming his way.

It was beginning to make a lot of sense to me.

Sonia

→≫·≪←

"I have a stack of children's books that need to be shelved. You want to work on that, Jamie?" Sonia asked when I arrived the next morning. I was hot and sweaty from the walk, even though it took less than ten minutes to get from my house to the library on foot.

"Sure. They're all picture books?" I asked. I had shelved a *lot* of picture books so far. Sonia saved them for me so there was always a stack waiting whether I arrived right at the ten o'clock opening or much later in the afternoon. Beverly told me I could choose my hours each day, that as long as I had fifteen by the end of the week, I was meeting my requirement. So I mixed it up.

"Mostly picture books, maybe some board books, I think. Beverly already checked them in." Sonia pointed me toward the pile on the cart behind her. It was a big pile. "But wipe the funky ones down first, please, with these." She pulled a container of antibacterial wipes out from under the counter and handed it to me.

I opened the container and the mixed scent of lemon and bleach hit me so hard my eyes watered. "You don't mess around, Sonia. This is some strong stuff," I said, pulling one wipe out of the small opening.

"Clean is good," she replied. "I like clean."

The first two books in the pile were brand-new, so I skipped them, but the next three had a smeared cloudy film all over their plastic covers. It came off right away with the wipes, though. I didn't even have to rub hard. The next book, a board book, was a different story.

"Uh, Sonia." I held it out in front of me with just two fingers, trying to touch it as little as possible. "There is no wet wipe in the world that can fix this one."

When Sonia looked at the book hanging from my fingertips, her mouth opened, her eyes softened, and her hand flew to her heart like a magnet to metal. "I haven't seen that book in so long!" she gushed.

I looked at the book again. The cover was stained and sticky, the corners were frayed, and the spine had a two-inch tear so the pages didn't line up evenly anymore.

Sonia took it from my hand and gazed at it lovingly. "This was my first book! I read it every day for weeks."

"It looks like a lot of other people read it, too," I said. "Or used it as a plate, or a Frisbee, or a sandbox toy."

"Hmm," Sonia said. "It does look pretty awful." She paused for a moment and then said, "But this book is so special to me."

"Really? *Colors and Shapes*?" I asked, doubt in my voice.

"Really." And then she explained, "I moved to Foxfield from Puerto Rico when I was six years old, and I didn't know a word of English. I spent my entire summer in this library, reading baby books over and over to learn English, and *Colors and Shapes* was the very first one I found and the very first one I mastered. This is *literally* the copy my little six-year-old hands held."

"You taught yourself English with baby books?"

"The children's room was like a second home to me." Sonia nodded. "And the Dewey decimal system was a language I understood before I understood English. I knew if I pulled a book off a shelf with a 567.9 on the spine it would be a dinosaur book, and if I grabbed one with a 398.2 it would be a fairy tale or folktale."

I smiled at the thought of little Sonia, sitting on the floor in a patch of sun with her legs crisscross applesauce, a stack of books like a friend at her side.

"So, what should we do with this, then? It's too damaged to go back on the shelf, right?" I asked.

"Right," Sonia agreed. "I'll put it in the discard stack downstairs and order a replacement."

"And then you should take it home, to keep. I can get *some* of the stains off for you, I think," I told her.

"Thank you, Jamie," Sonia said. "I'd love that."

I wheeled my cart of books and the wet wipes into the children's room to work, since the front desk was getting busy with patron traffic.

I placed Sonia's book to the side while I worked on cleaning and drying the others. Then I organized them in alphabetical order on the cart so they would be easier to shelve.

I was almost finished with the last of the *W*s when the cover of a book caught my eye. On it, a red fox was leaping after two terrified rabbits, and the title was printed like a banner in bright colors across the middle of the cover. It immediately made me think of my Foxfield Elementary School yearbook.

Every spring there was a contest to design the cover of that year's K–5 yearbook. Any fifth grader could enter a drawing into the contest. A committee of teachers and PTA members narrowed the entries down to three, and then all the fifth graders got to vote for the winner. The voting and the winning announcement all happened on the same day.

"You better enter," Vic told me back in fifth grade once the announcement was made to submit entries. "I'll kill you if you don't enter."

"You won't *kill* me," I said back.

"Fine, I won't," she admitted, "but I *will* steal the corn chips out of your lunch every day, and Aunt Julie's special brownies, when you have them."

"You already do that." I poked her.

"Then I'll do it even more." Vic poked me back.

"She hasn't made those in a while." Aunt Julie's brownies were heaven—she put chocolate chips in them *and* on top of them, with rainbow sprinkles, too, which gave them the perfect crunch.

"So you have two jobs tonight—draw a yearbook cover and call your aunt," Vic ordered.

"Fine," I said. "But a lot of people enter, and there are a lot of other good artists."

"But you're the best," Vic said, her voice full of confidence.

I did enter the contest, along with half our class and lots of kids in the other fifth-grade classes, too.

I could remember the morning assembly perfectly, when the final three submissions were announced. My drawing made the cut, so I was called up to the stage and had to stand beside Pratik Bhatt and Trina Evans while our drawings were displayed one at a time on a huge screen. All three designs were good, but I definitely heard the audience ooh and aah the most over mine. I knew it didn't matter, though. Trina was the most popular girl in the whole grade, and popularity always won. Pratik and I weren't really even in the running. And the proud look on Trina's face showed that she knew it. She had it in the bag.

But then it happened.

The principal announced that the committee had decided to change the procedure this year. There would be no voting. The winner had already been determined. Then the screen went wild crazy, flashing the three designs over and over while the principal crooned into her microphone, "And the winner is . . ."

The room got quiet, more silent than a fire drill.

The flashing stopped.

And then all that was left was the image of my drawing, bright and huge, a fox wearing a Foxfield T-shirt leaping toward a banner with the name of our school and the year printed on it in swirly 3D letters. The room went silent, then erupted in hoots and shouts and clapping. I'd won! I couldn't believe it! A smile so wide it almost hurt spread across my face as I scanned the auditorium and tried to find Vic in the crowd.

"Congrats," Pratik leaned over to tell me before he left the stage. "Your drawing really is the best."

"Thanks," I answered, still trying to process what had just happened. "Yours is really good, too."

And then I saw Trina, her lips clamped together, a pink flush creeping up her cheeks as she stood stiffly in her brand-new dress, bought just for the occasion. Her smirk was long gone, replaced by something threatening and scary. She caught me looking at her and shot me a furious glare. Then she flipped her hair and walked offstage, back to her group of friends, all of them clearing a spot for her to sit next to them.

I shook the principal's hand and started slowly back to my seat. Trina's anger had stomped my happiness away. I guessed I could understand why she was so mad. It wasn't fair that the year they decided to get rid of the voting was the same year Trina had a chance to be the cover designer. But it wasn't *my* fault. Trina should have been mad at the committee, not at me.

But I wasn't about to explain that to her.

Two years later, she still had it out for me. And without meaning to, I had given her the perfect chance to get even. And then some.

"I'm done with the kids' books," I told Sonia, pushing the empty cart back to her, "except this one needs a new label. It's ripped."

"Thanks, mami," she said, then mentioned, "Some girls your age were in here yesterday." She was working on the computer, making a record set of old magazines to discard.

I met her eyes.

"You were here," she continued, "but seemed to be busy at the time." It seemed like she was aware that I was only busy avoiding those girls.

"Lots of girls my age come in here," I responded, trying to dodge.

"Actually, not true at all. The twelve-to-sixteen age group, boys *and* girls, is who we see the very least of in this building."

Sonia knew everything about the library. She knew the history of the building, the titles in the collection, the delivery times for each magazine, the dates of upcoming events weeks in advance, and, unfortunately for me, the statistics of local library users.

I let out a sigh. "I probably didn't know them."

"You were hiding from them." Sonia cut to the chase.

I winced.

Sonia stared at me, waiting.

"Maybe I was," I admitted.

"Clearly not friends of yours," Sonia stated next.

"Clearly," I agreed. My cheeks began to flush and my stupid eyes began to water. I blinked furiously to fight back the tears.

Sonia took a long look at me, then turned back to the screen to continue working on her magazine record set.

"Makes sense," she finally said. "They seemed bottom shelf to me."

I couldn't hide a smile at that, but it disappeared quickly as I relived what I'd overheard yesterday in my head: Trina, Izzy, and Amanda laughing about me.

"You look down," Sonia said, little lines of worry squirming across her forehead.

I shrugged but didn't deny it.

"How about our game? You wanna play?"

I looked around the room. The library had emptied out a bit while I was working in the children's room.

"I dare you," she challenged me, and she did this thing with her eyebrows so they moved up and down really quickly.

It made me laugh.

"Okay." I grabbed a pencil and scrap paper and ran to the back room, wrote a few things down, then returned to Sonia with her first challenge. "How about *The Best American Short Stories of the Century*, call number 813.010805."

Sonia had a photographic memory. She could tell you the exact location of a title in the stacks, whether it was an audiobook, a regular book, or a DVD. To pass time during slow hours, we made a game of testing her on it.

"Back room, third stack from the left, fourth shelf down in the middle," she answered without even a pause to think.

She was right.

"Okay, how about *The Omnivore's Dilemma*, call number 394.12."

"Back room. Second stack from the right, middle shelf, third row from the top," she answered quickly, then took a sip of coffee. Her mug said *Book Lovers Never Go to Bed Alone*.

"Right again!" I told her. "Wow, you're good."

"And the spine is a yellowy-gold," Sonia added, and then winked at me.

My jaw dropped open, just a little bit. She was scary good.

JULY

Wally

⇢⇉⋅⇇⇠

It was Monday morning, bright and *hot as the dickens*, an expression Beverly taught me at the same time that she pointed out a Charles Dickens quote on Black Hat Guy's chair: *I have been bent and broken, but—I hope—into a better shape.* I hadn't read any Charles Dickens yet, but I certainly could relate to feeling bent and broken.

The air-conditioning window units were churning full force when Wally arrived just a few minutes after opening.

"Good morning to you, and a good morning it is," he announced, then stopped in his tracks to look around the building, studying the space as if seeing it for the very first time.

"Never been here on a Monday before," he finally said. Then he released a loud, heavy breath and exclaimed, "Looks exactly the same!" He threw his head back and laughed, sounding a lot like a choking train slowly rolling into the station for repairs.

Wally coughed, cleared his throat, and asked, "Can you believe the Fourth of July had the nerve to fall on a Tuesday and mess with my schedule?"

"The nerve!" Sonia played along, then said, "It was bound to happen eventually. We're truly sorry to be closed on your day."

"Ah, well, I forgive you," he raised his pointer finger above his head and finished, "*this time!*" He chuckled again, then went to his vase and took out the yellow carnation. I had wanted to pull it days ago. By last Thursday its petals were shriveled and browned at the edges; by Friday its entire flower face had folded over onto its stem.

"Can't we put this thing out of its misery?" I had asked Sonia Friday afternoon, lifting it out of the glass jar.

"No, Jamie. It means a lot to Wally. Leave it for him to do."

I plucked off one grungy petal and dropped the flower back in. "All right," I agreed.

"Just try not to look at it." She shuddered.

Wally reached around the circulation desk and dropped the dead flower in our trash can, something he had never done before. He usually bagged his old flower and took it home with his new movie selections. He reached his doughy pink hand into his bag and came out with three white carnations this time instead of his usual one.

He slipped each of them into the jar.

"There you go now," he said. "Could probably use some new water."

"I'll take care of it, Wally," Sonia told him right away.

"I got three flowers today. A little different from my usual," he said.

"What's the occasion?"

"No occasion. No occasion at all, actually. Opposite of occasion," he answered.

"Wally, that is a cryptic answer," Sonia challenged him.

"Oh, I got canceled on, that's all," he answered, waving his hand to the side as if pushing away a bad thought.

"Oh no. Who canceled?"

"My kids." Wally shrugged as he said it. "They were supposed to come over. We had a date and I got 'em both a flower, my boy and my girl, but then they couldn't make it."

"That's disappointing. I'm sorry," Sonia said, her voice softening. "Is everything okay?"

"Oh yeah, sure. Nothing like that. They're just busy, you know? And it's an hour drive each way for them, so—" He turned his head and coughed, and coughed.

And coughed.

I expected to see a piece of lung on the floor by the time he finished.

Sonia held her ground patiently, waiting for him to finish his phlegm attack. "It's hard for them to get away," he continued once he recovered. "They've got jobs and kids of their own, you know?"

"Ay, I know, Wally." She nodded.

"So busy when you're young," Wally continued. "Too busy for dates with dear old dad."

"Well, we are very happy to have all three of your beautiful flowers, Wally. They brighten up this whole room." Sonia gave him a genuine smile, and the room really did seem to brighten up just then. It could have been the flowers, or it could have been Sonia's smile.

Because Sonia was gorgeous.

Completely and totally gorgeous.

Sonia had the most stunningly silky black hair I'd ever seen in my whole life. My hair looked like wispy, dried-out straw next to hers, all thin and straight and lackluster brown next to her glossy midnight tresses. Her lips were painted the same shade of soft pink every day, popping against her tan skin. And her eyelashes were long. Seriously long. There were times I wondered about some of the people who came in to "browse the collection." I suspected they were there just as much to snatch glimpses of Sonia.

Wally turned to me. "And how are you today, dear?" he

asked, looking me square in the eyes.

"I'm good. I mean, I'm doing well today. Thanks for asking." I noticed that he didn't look well at all, though. Being stood up by his own kids must have really messed with him. His hair looked greasier than normal, his skin was patchy, and his eyes looked watery.

"Do you have some DVDs for me?" I asked.

"Of course, yeah, yeah. Got my flicks right here." Wally reached back into his plastic bag and extracted five cases, all rubber-banded together. "Here you go, young lady. Here you go."

"Thank you." I walked them over to Sonia and she began scanning them in.

"You know what it's like, then, too, being so young and busy?" Wally said to me. He couldn't let it go, like he wanted someone to confirm for him that his grown children had had no choice but to cancel on him. He didn't want to face that they might have just ditched him, plain and simple. "How old are you then? Fifteen?"

"I'm thirteen," I said, flattered that he thought I was older. I probably just looked older because I was standing behind the counter. *Context clues*, my language arts teacher would say.

"Only thirteen?" Wally laughed at his guess, and his laugh morphed into a cough. He draped his whole forearm over the counter for support and coughed deep and long and with enough force to move furniture. It was a good thing the circulation desk was bolted to the floor.

Sonia's eyebrows pinched together and she moved briskly to the watercooler to get him a drink. As I watched her go I saw one patron, an older woman in a long floral sundress, grimace at the sounds coming out of Wally.

Wally righted himself and wiped his mouth on his sleeve.

"Thirteen, huh?" Wally stated again, absorbing this fact. "So you still live with your dear old dad?"

"I live with my mom. Just the two of us," I explained.

"Oh, sorry, dear," Wally apologized automatically.

"No, don't be sorry," I reassured him. "It's great, just my mom and me. I love it that way."

"You do?" he asked.

Sonia was back and paying attention now, I saw.

"Yes. It's always been just the two of us. I don't remember my dad at all. And my mom says that's not a bad thing, considering."

"Considering what?" Sonia was more than curious now.

"Considering we couldn't squeeze him."

"What's that?" Sonia asked.

"We couldn't squeeze him." I smiled at the confusion spreading over Sonia's face, and then explained, "That's how my mom explained it to me when I was little, why she left him and why he let us go. We couldn't make lemonade out of the lemon of him. We couldn't squeeze out anything good or sweet."

"Your mom compared your dad to a lemon?" Sonia asked.

"As a dad, yes, and a husband, yeah, because he was. She said he had his good points, like he's the reason I've always been in the advanced math track at school, and he's the reason I'm good at art, and why I have a dimple on just one side. But she said he didn't have a single caretaking bone in his whole body. So as a dad—a lemon."

"How about that," Wally said, thinking it through.

"My mom said his one true goal in life revealed everything she needed to know about him."

"And what was that goal?" Sonia asked.

"To make as much money as possible, doing the least amount of work possible."

"Huh," Wally grunted.

"She did meet him in a casino," I added.

"Touché," Sonia responded.

"Anyway, once she figured that out, she knew he wasn't the kind of role model she wanted for me and he wasn't the kind of guy she wanted to spend her life with, so she made the second-best decision of her life: leaving him."

"And what was the first-best decision?" Sonia asked.

"Falling for him long enough to make me." I smiled when I said that. I couldn't *not* smile when I said it.

Sonia's face broke into a smile, too.

"I think I really like your mom," she told me.

Which made me smile even more. I liked that Sonia and my mom had the single-parent thing in common. Sonia had her son, Mateo, who was grown and beginning graduate school, and my mom had me.

"Well, I bet you and your mom watch movies together all the time," Wally said.

"Sometimes we do," I answered, not sure if that was going to make him feel bad or not. I balanced it with "But we live together, so it's easy. We don't have to drive an hour to get to each other. We just fit it in whenever it works out."

"Ah, those good ole days," Wally said out loud, even though it looked like he was taking a private trip in his mind back to the time when his kids were little and still lived with him. Then he snapped out of it and said, "All right then."

He turned from me back to Sonia and said, "You better watch those child labor laws, this one's only thirteen." He pointed at me with his thick, swollen fingers and laughed again.

Please, I thought, *don't laugh*. I didn't want him to start coughing again, because of the sundress lady still searching the shelf and because the coughing fits seemed to get worse each time.

"I didn't think you could work, actually, if you're only thirteen. Legally, I mean," Wally shared.

"Well, I don't really *work* here. I, um . . . I . . . ," I faltered. The familiar flush of pink heat started creeping up my neck to my cheeks.

"She's a volunteer." Sonia swooped in and saved me. "Have a sip, Wally. Your throat sounds dry." She handed him the paper cup.

He swallowed the water in one gulp and dropped the cup into his plastic bag. "I'll use that cup again at home. Thank you, dear," he said to Sonia. "And good for you to volunteer." Wally spoke to me now. "Didn't know kids did that anymore."

"We're lucky to have her," Sonia said, and winked at me. "Your movies are all checked in, Wally. You can go hunt for your new ones for the week."

"Let me know if you need help finding anything," I added. I had heard Sonia and Beverly and Lenny say this to patrons, but this was the first time I'd said it. I liked the way the words sounded coming out of my mouth. It sounded like I really could help somebody. Like I really could find a title Wally was looking for and take it to the checkout desk for him and send him on his way with exactly what he'd come to the library for.

I liked the idea of being able to help Wally, or any patron who needed help. The right way.

Because the last time I tried to help someone, I did it the wrong way.

The last time, I just took a book off the shelf, slipped it under my hoodie, and walked.

Straight to Trey's backpack.

Lenny

–»»·«««–

On Wednesday, Lenny was crouched over Black Hat Guy in his quotes chair, his hand on the shoulder that may or may not have been shaking under the heavy sweatshirt. Black Hat Guy's face was chalk white.

It must have been a really bad dream. I was upstairs in the loft, a smallish room that housed the fiction collection and a few study cubicles, when I heard the noise. There was quiet grumbling first, then louder groaning, and then a second later Black Hat Guy was full-on shouting while one leg jerked and kicked like he was trying to shake something off it, his eyes still shut in sleep the whole time.

Lenny got to him first, at the exact moment Black Hat Guy jerked too hard and pulled his charging wire out of the wall socket. The whole outlet came out of the wall with it, the screws caked with dried plaster, a small cloud of white dust raining down on the carpet below. Black Hat Guy popped up from his slumped sleeping position like a jack-in-the-box and reached frantically for the plug end of his charging wire. Lenny reached out to soothe him.

"You're in the library and you're all right," Lenny said to him, over and over. "You're in the library and it's all good, man. You're in the library and you're all right." It almost sounded like an old folk song, the way Lenny said it.

Beverly stood a few feet behind Lenny, running her hands down her corduroy pants, looking like she wanted to help but giving Lenny space to try first.

After a few minutes of this, Black Hat Guy started to relax and slumped back into his turtle posture. His neck retracted into his bulky sweatshirt. His breathing slowed.

I was walking behind the circulation desk to return cleaning supplies when Lenny noticed me and called, "Hey there, Jamie. Think you could get us a drink of water?"

Lenny was kneeling now beside the chair, his hand still on Black Hat Guy's shoulder. He smiled at me encouragingly.

I headed straight to the watercooler outside Beverly's office. Bubbles glugged up as I pushed the button in and watched cold water pour into a tissue-thin paper cup.

Lenny took the cup from me. "Thank you, Jamie. This is

excellent." He handed it to Black Hat Guy carefully. "Here you go, man. Nature's wine."

Black Hat Guy took a careful sip, then said, "Nature's wine is actually wine, I think." His voice was shaky but his face looked normal again, the bits of it you could see, at least.

"Yeah, you're probably right about that," Lenny laughed. Beverly laughed, too, which made Lenny turn and realize for the first time that she was right behind him. I walked back to the circ desk to stand with Sonia.

"I think we're doing okay now, Beverly. We're looking good," Lenny told her.

"Okay, great." Beverly looked relieved and nodded in approval. "Is there anything I can get you?" she asked anyway.

"We're all good, right, man?" Lenny asked Black Hat Guy.

"Yeah, sorry, though. Sorry for the racket," he mumbled, addressing Beverly without looking up at her. The way he said it, and the way he was all slumped in his chair with his head down, made me think of the day I sat in Mrs. Shupe's office, offering my own apology, slumped the same shameful way in one of her hard wooden chairs.

"Oh, no, no, it's okay. It's no problem. I'm glad everything's okay now. Just let me know if you need anything," Beverly offered. She smiled at Black Hat Guy and smiled at Lenny and then headed back to her office, nodding to the few patrons she passed on her way, telling them, "Everything's fine. I apologize for the disturbance. Everything's okay."

"Must have been one banger of a dream," Lenny said to Black Hat Guy.

"Yeah, well. I have that one a lot. Keeps coming back."

"I hear you," Lenny told him, giving his shoulder a small squeeze. "I hear that."

Lenny and Black Hat Guy continued to talk quietly while I stood by Sonia, who was busy checking circulation statistics on the computer. I could only see the back of Lenny from where I stood. The hair on the top of his head was so thin you could see scalp peeking through, but his ponytail of wiry brown and gray hair hung a good ten inches down his back. He was wearing another one of his thin peasant tops made out of hemp. He had already explained to me how that cloth was made from the hemp plant, and how you could eat hemp, too. It seemed strange that something you could eat could also be turned into something you could wear, but I didn't doubt him. He knew a ton about plants and loved putting healthy ingredients in the treats he brought to the library for us. Lenny really liked to feed people and take care of them. "Best way to help yourself is to help others," he had told me several times already, like it was his own personal motto.

Which was probably why he was the first to get to Black

Hat Guy when his nightmare burst the seams of his brain and shattered all over the library.

"That was weird," I said to Sonia quietly.

"I've seen weirder," she said back, not missing a beat.

I raised my eyebrows at her.

"I've worked here twenty-some years now," she told me, cupping her mug of steaming coffee with both hands. "Trust me, I could write a book."

"Are you going to?" I asked, completely serious.

"Ay Dios mío," she said, shaking her head. "I'm a writer now? What, with all my free time?" She tsk-tsked at me. "There are lots of people out there with stories to tell, anyway. I bet his is a doozy." She nodded toward Black Hat Guy.

I looked at Black Hat Guy again. He looked like a kid hunkered down in his sleeping bag, hiding from the screeches and creaks of the dark outdoors around him.

Lenny kept talking and Black Hat Guy kept listening and responding.

"I've never seen him talk to anybody before. Ever," I told Sonia.

"Everyone talks to Lenny," Sonia said. "He's like the bartender of libraries."

Lenny looked over then, as if he had heard his name. He smiled at me quickly but then rested his eyes on Sonia. A sudden warmth glowed from his skin, and his face seemed to open up as he gazed at her.

I knew that look.

I knew that feeling.

That was me whenever I saw Trey. Tall, lanky, artsy Trey, with his velvety dark hair and his tiny tan mole under his left eye and his sketchbook clutched like a life preserver to his chest. Trey, who just *had* to be Trina's older brother, who just *had* to smell like the most perfect mix of pencil shavings and cinnamon, who just *had* to tell his friend how worried he was about his language arts final on *Jane Eyre* when I was sitting right behind him at Art Club.

I heard the concern in his voice. I couldn't get it out of my head.

Trey.

And I could see now that Sonia was Lenny's Trey. Lenny's face said it all. He was crazy in love with her. Maybe that was why he said Foxfield was a good place to be. Maybe Sonia was why he was "staying put."

Sonia caught Lenny staring and turned back to her computer screen, shaking her head slowly.

Working at the library just got a little more interesting.

Black Hat Guy

→>>>·<<<·

Lightning crackled across the sky and thunder boomed loud and sudden. It was Friday afternoon and we hadn't had rain in weeks. The sky ripped open and gigantic drops, heavy and cold, fell with such force they bounced back up from the pavement. I was behind the library, emptying the metal book-drop containers, totally unprepared for rain.

Luckily, there were only five books in the drop. I shoved them under my shirt and quickly worked to secure the book-drop doors, twisting the combination locks like Beverly had showed me, before hightailing it back into the library. One raindrop found its way under my shirt collar. It snaked down my back, leaving a trail of chill that made me shiver.

As I struggled to wipe the water off my back, I noticed Black Hat Guy headed my way, weaving through the cars in the parking lot behind the library. He was moving quickly, and for the first time his sweatshirt, jeans, and hat made perfect sense for the weather. He was hunched over, as always, his stuffed backpack hanging off one shoulder like it was just another part of his body.

I reached the front door the same time as Black Hat Guy. While I struggled to get a hand out from under my shirt where I was protecting the books, Black Hat Guy pulled open the door. He held it open while the rain pelted him and, looking down at his feet, muttered, "After you."

I hurried into the dry library. The cold of the AC brought goose bumps to my arms and legs instantly. Black Hat Guy followed me in and sighed like a weary traveler who had finally arrived home. He dripped his way to his chair, leaned his backpack against it, and plugged in his phone to charge. Drops of water sprayed from the tips of his boots with each step he took. He helped himself to several paper towels by the watercooler and proceeded to wipe down his jeans and sweatshirt, front and back, before returning to his chair.

"Oh no, Jamie, the rain got you?" Beverly asked, approaching me with concern.

"Yes, but it's fine. There were only a few books." I pulled them out from under my shirt for her to see. "They look pretty good."

"Great job. Thank you." Beverly smiled at me. "Let's not empty the book drops again until the rain stops, okay?"

"Okay, I won't," I said, proud that these five books looked okay. I had already been schooled, on my very first day at the library, about the dangers of water. Beverly had explained that water was the absolute worst thing for books. I couldn't help thinking fire must be at least as bad, but I hadn't mentioned it. It had been my first day, after all.

"Well, Sonia can check those in, and we'll just have to look carefully at any returns now, for water damage," Beverly told us. She looked at the pile of used paper towels on the floor by Black Hat Guy's feet and announced, "I'll go get extra paper towels."

I handed the books over to Sonia. "You might want to dry off, Jamie. Your hair is dripping." She took a handful of hair off my back and lifted it in front of my eyes so I could see the rain collecting on the ends, spheres of water hanging like glass ornaments, then falling silently to the tile floor.

"Here." She reached into her purse under the desk and came out with a comb. "Use this." She handed it to me. "There's a mirror downstairs by the sink."

"That's okay. I'm fine," I said, squeezing some water out of my hair.

"You're not *looking* fine at all. Go clean up. It's important to look professional." She thrust her comb at me again, then winked and said, "Besides, you never know who might show up here."

My mouth opened in response, but nothing came out. How much did she know about me and why I was working at the library this summer?

"Hurry, go. I may need your help with wet books soon." Sonia waved me out of her way.

As soon as I saw my reflection in the mirror downstairs, I knew Sonia was right. Even without the rainstorm, I was a mess. I hadn't combed my hair after rolling out of bed that morning and I had yellow bags under my eyes. My skin was sickly pale, which made perfect sense considering all the nights I spent in my room drawing until two o'clock in the morning and all the days I spent either inside the library or hiding at home. I didn't want to see anyone, and I didn't want anyone to see me. Even my short walk to and from the library each day had me on high alert, my heart pounding in my ears in fear of having to face anyone from school. Vic was at camp for the *entire* summer, and I didn't have any other friends. I had people I was friendly *with*, but they all quietly drifted away once I became the most-talked-about girl in my grade.

Our middle school Honor Code was long-standing, but it wasn't like no one ever cheated. It wasn't like the Honor Code hadn't been broken before. Earlier this year, cheat sheets were found in a couple of hallway trash cans right after midterm exams. The evidence was clear—answer sheets that matched the tests perfectly—but the teachers weren't able to prove who had used them. So no one ever got in trouble for it.

No one got caught. Ever.

Until me.

The one time in my whole little life I did something so *not me* at school, so totally *un-Jamie*-like, and it had to become a school-wide scandal.

It had to blow up in my face in the most public way possible.

("Our Honor Code cannot be disrespected," Mrs. Shupe had said back in her office that Wednesday in May. "I'm sure you're aware of the violations that occurred earlier in the year and the difficulties they presented. We were unable to pinpoint the culprits, which makes your position now particularly . . . unfortunate." She paused, then her voice became more forceful as she said, as if to an auditorium full of people, "The message to the student body must be loud and clear. There is a zero tolerance policy for this kind of behavior. Helping someone cheat is just as bad as cheating yourself.")

I wished I could jump right to the library hours—it sounded much better than facing a whole month of school with everyone talking about me, laughing at me, staring me down in the hallway. From the moment I stepped out of the principal's office, every whisper I heard seemed to be about me.

Then Trina made her move, and it got even worse.

She did it on Thursday, May 25, exactly one day after my meeting with Mrs. Shupe.

Vic was waiting for me at my locker at the end of the day, same as always, but the look on her face when I got there made my mouth go dry and my skin feel prickly with heat. She didn't say a word. She just lifted her cell phone to my face so I could see what was on the screen. So I could read what *everybody* was reading.

All I had to see was the first line to know exactly what it was.

"No" came out of me like a dying breath. My stomach cramped and my vision went wobbly and I wanted to evaporate on the spot.

For the first time ever, Vic couldn't come up with any reassuring words to say to me. She knew how bad this was.

I raced home from school and called my mom at her office, begging her to leave work early. Then I collapsed on the kitchen table, sobbing into my arms until I was nothing but a heap of pink puffy eyes and crumpled used tissues.

My mom made it home in ten minutes flat.

"Oh, Jamie," she said gently, pushing my hair off my

forehead. "I told you this would be the hard part, these first few days of facing everyone while it's still fresh. But it'll fade and people won't care anymore, you'll see."

"She posted it."

"What?" My mom's forehead wrinkled up. "Who posted it? Posted what?"

"Trina. My letter." I could only get out a few words at a time between sobs. "My apology. To Trey."

"She posted it?"

"Yes. Everyone saw it. *Everyone* read it." I used the bottom of my shirt to wipe my eyes. "They all know."

"Oh no."

My mom had encouraged me to write and deliver the apology letter the day it was assigned, so I could at least get one weight off my back. She had also encouraged me to be honest. Mrs. Shupe wasn't going to see it. She only needed confirmation from Trey that he received it. So I took my mom's advice and was honest. Very honest. I explained in the letter that I never intended to get him in trouble, that I was only trying to help him with his final because I cared about him, because I liked him so much. Because I had liked him for a long time. Because he was so nice. And smart. And talented. And really cute. And I couldn't put it into words perfectly—but I just felt *connected* to him in some way, like maybe we were meant to be.

I wrote all of that.

And now the whole world knew. Now I was the cheater *and* the desperate loser getting in major trouble for a boy who didn't even like her back.

I was a total laughingstock.

My mom didn't say a word. She just pulled a chair out, sat next to me, and stroked my hair.

"I can't go back," I finally said, my voice muffled in the crook of my arm. "I can't."

"Well, you have to go back. You know that."

"Thanks, Mom. Thank you so much for the comfort." I lifted my head to look at her. Maybe if she saw the true suffering in my face, she'd agree to call me in sick for a few days, maybe a week, maybe two.

"This is the hand you dealt yourself, and now you have to play it," was her response.

She wasn't going to call me in sick.

"You know, Trina's going to get in trouble for doing that, for posting it," my mom said.

"So what? That doesn't *undo* it," I huffed. "*Everyone knows.* I'm totally humiliated."

"Forget the summer assignment, honey. I think the real punishment is right here, right now, until school lets out in June."

"I don't have to do the summer assignment?" I asked, hopeful.

"Of course you do. Every single hour of it. I'm just saying the worst part is *now*, facing everyone, every day, until school ends."

I pushed back in my chair, pulled my knees up to my chin, and hugged my shins to me. "So what am I supposed to do? How am I supposed to get through this?"

"You have Vic."

"I have Vic for only three classes a day. I have no one for the other five."

My mom let this sink in. She twirled the bracelet on her wrist, a string bracelet I had made her when I was ten that she never took off.

Finally she said, "Well then, duck feathers."

"Huh?"

"Duck feathers," she repeated, as if it were self-explanatory.

"Again, huh?" I asked, trying to be patient.

"Ducks secrete a waxy oil onto their feathers—"

"Gross, Mom." I made a face.

"Jamie," my mom scolded, not trying to be patient at all.

"You said 'secrete.' Is there even a grosser word out there?"

"Ducks have feathers covered in a waxy oil," she continued, ignoring my question, "that makes them completely waterproof.

In the water and out. Even if they're in a lake and there's rain pouring down on them, water rolls off their backs. It doesn't get to them, the real them, underneath. They stay dry and protected—the rain can't hurt them. You have to be like that."

"I have to be like a wet duck?"

"You have to let it roll off your back." She took my hand in hers and held it. "The stares, the teasing, the judgments. Let it all roll off your back."

"Mom, I'm in middle school," I reminded her.

"I know, Jamie."

"So that's, like, the most unhelpful advice ever."

"Maybe, but you'll keep it in your head anyway, and eventually, you *will* value these words."

"Really? I'll value the words 'feathers' and 'duck'?"

"Yes," she said, and squeezed my hand once, then released it. "Someday. You will."

"Someday," I repeated, not even for a mini-second believing it.

"Now let's order Chinese food. I'm starving."

So, as I stood there looking at my reflection in the library staff mirror, it was clear that Sonia was right. I looked really bad. I looked like someone who was very alone. And I looked completely and entirely unprofessional. And that had to change.

I got to work. I combed every tangle out of my hair and

parted it on the side, sweeping half behind my right ear. Because it was wet, it stayed there, as if it had been shellacked into place. I pinched my cheeks to get some color in them, a trick I learned from watching the movie *Sense and Sensibility* with my mom.

I decided right then to take Sonia's advice to heart. I would come to the library from now on looking professional, like a real library employee. Like someone you could trust with a book.

I grabbed a paper towel and squeezed more water out of the ends of my hair. Then I took one last look at myself in the mirror. My shirt was still spotted with raindrops, but there was nothing I could do about that. Those would fade. My hair looked better. I promised myself right then, while staring at my reflection, that I would start getting more sleep, too.

And it was precisely then that I realized: I'd been so surprised to hear Black Hat Guy speak, when he stood patiently in the rain and held the door open for me, that I'd never even said, "Thank you."

I had to do better. It was only the beginning of July, so I had plenty of time to improve. I would start fresh on Monday. I would be like Sonia, friendly and helpful. I would be nicely dressed with brushed hair.

And I would remember to say thank you.

Beverly

→→→·←←←

"I thought you might be up here," Beverly said as she reached the top of the staircase to the loft. Because the library's cleaning service budget had been cut in half, I had decided to dust the shelves, tables, and handrails every Monday morning to get the building ready for a busy week.

"I'm almost done wiping down the study cubicles," I told her. "I already finished the shelves."

"It really looks great up here, Jamie," Beverly said, scanning the space, nodding her approval. "Just tip-top."

"Thanks." I went back to wiping.

"If you don't mind, I'd like you to come downstairs, please. I have another job for you."

"Sure," I answered, and followed her down the steps.

She walked me to the returns cart behind the circulation

desk. "I'd like you to work on these now." She rested her hand on a stack of audiobook cases.

"Okay. Um, you want me to clean them?" I guessed.

"No. I want you to shelve them." She handed me one from the pile.

"But I thought I wasn't allowed to shelve adult stuff. You know," I reminded her, "in case I make a mistake. You wanted me to only straighten up and shelf-read."

"That was before. You've done an excellent job here the past few weeks, and I'm confident you can handle this new task."

"Wow. Thanks." I flushed a little. "Okay, so do these now?"

"Yes. And if you need any help or get stuck, just ask Sonia."

Sonia turned then from the computer to wink at me. "The audiobooks are very straightforward, Jamie. It's a good place to start."

"Okay. Thank you," I said again. I picked three from the cart and headed toward the audiobook wall.

"Jamie, push the whole cart there. You'll go crazy walking back and forth." Sonia rolled her eyes at me. "The carts are on wheels, remember?" She laughed at me then, but it was a non-mean, we're-all-in-this-together, supportive laugh.

It wasn't a that's-the-pathetic-girl-who-wrote-the-love-letter laugh.

I knew exactly how *that* laugh sounded—I had heard it over and over at school.

I pushed the cart with more effort than I expected to need—it rolled like a deformed supermarket cart—and counted the items on it. There were nineteen audiobooks. This would take Sonia about three minutes, but it took me fifteen. As I read each call number and carefully searched for its spot on the shelf, I found myself almost having fun. Every item had its home, its own place to belong. It was just like Sonia said—everything made sense in the library. There was a language that was easy to understand and an order that was easy to follow inside these walls. My colossal mistake at school, my bad judgment, my humiliation all faded away while I worked, and all I felt was the nice satisfaction of putting things back in order, of making things right.

Beverly liked her library neat and precise and pinpoint accurate, and she was trusting *me* with that. She might as well have been handing me her newborn baby.

After I shelved all nineteen audiobooks, I stood back to admire my work. The wall looked full and organized and perfectly straight. Then I got paranoid that I might have made a mistake, so I shelf-read the entire wall. Again.

Shelf reading was pretty much the most un-fun and tedious job in the whole entire world. It meant reading the call numbers on the spine labels one at a time, to make sure they were all in the correct order. Call numbers could get pretty long and complicated, like 941.0081, 941.00812, 941.00821. After reading a dozen of those, your head started to spin and the numbers blurred, and before you knew it you couldn't remember if two came before five or after, or if four was a number or a letter. It sounded stupid, but trust me, shelf reading could make even the most brainiac person bleary in a very short amount of time.

Pushing the empty cart back to the circ desk took me right past Beverly's office. Her door was open a few inches, and in that small gap I caught her sitting at her desk, staring at something small she held in both hands. A gold chain, threaded around her pinkie finger, dangled down over her keyboard.

Her necklace.

She had taken it off and was gently rubbing a fingertip over the front, like rubbing a lamp to summon the genie inside. Then she opened it up. It was a locket! There was probably a photo of someone special inside. She gazed at it, quiet and still, so frozen in thought she looked like she was holding a pose, as if an artist were set up on the other side of her desk, scratching away on a canvas with pencil to catch her image.

Beverly took a sudden deep breath, snapped the locket shut, and clasped it back around her neck. She scanned the contents of her small, spare office, then directed her attention to her desk and adjusted the lamp, laptop, tissue box, and penholder so they all sat perfectly square on the tabletop. Before she could notice me spying on her, I quickly cast my eyes down to the cart in front of me and pushed it back to Sonia.

Who was in Beverly's locket? She wasn't married or divorced and didn't have any kids, and she never mentioned any boyfriend or girlfriend. When Beverly opened that locket and peered inside so intensely, I saw myself, alone in my bedroom, opening the middle school yearbook to stare at Trey.

He was pictured with his homeroom on page twelve, sitting on a desk, staring right at the camera in his black Vincent van Gogh T-shirt. All the homeroom shots that year were the *silly* photos that the photographer always promised to take after getting a few good, serious ones. In those shots, there were always a few kids who still tried to give their best smile, a few who wouldn't cooperate at all, and the rest who let loose: tongues out, eyes crossed, arms flailing, fingers up noses.

Trey wasn't silly in the *silly* photo, though. He just focused on the camera, waited for the click, and then probably whipped his sketchbook out the moment the photographer was done so he could get back to whatever drawing he was working on. He was always drawing something.

His solo school portrait was on page twenty-eight. He wore a brown collared shirt, the brown matching the molten chocolaty shade of his eyes perfectly, and he smiled softly at the camera. His eyelashes were the reach-out-and-grab-you kind like Sonia's. I lost myself staring at that picture, pretending that his smile wasn't for the photographer or for his mom, who told him to cooperate because she had to prepay, but was for me.

Just for me.

I guessed if I had a locket, that's the picture I would keep inside, always with me, safe and tucked in right above my heart.

Maybe Beverly had a picture of her middle school crush in that locket and the reason she was a single, overworked, middle-aged librarian today was because she was still stuck on that one person.

That's what Vic would say, at least, because she liked to tease me about Trey. It was an easy poke for her, since I couldn't get her back.

"Fortunately for me, there isn't a single specimen in our entire town that I find even remotely appealing," she loved to tell me.

And it was true. She had never had a crush on anyone. Yet.

I wasn't even sure how I could still like Trey so much after all the trouble my crush on him had caused me. Vic couldn't help me understand it, either. She just said, "The heart wants what it wants," and threw her arm around my shoulders, giving me a firm squeeze in support.

"You did *not* just say that to me," I challenged her, narrowing my eyes.

She laughed and waved me off. "I heard it on this horrendous soap opera my mom watches." And then she acted it out, lifting her hand to her brow and gazing off into the distance as she repeated, but this time in some made-up accent, "The heart wants what it wants."

"Well, *my* heart wants to go back in time and redo a particular day," I said.

"*My* heart wants a mega KitKat bar," Vic said back.

So I would wear a photo of Trey in my locket and Vic would wear a photo of a candy bar.

As for what photo Beverly had hidden inside her locket, I had absolutely no idea.

Trina

➤➤➤·◄◄◄

When Sonia asked me to display the new stack of *Biweekly* newsletters in the reading room on Wednesday, I couldn't help but notice one of the front-page headlines: *Eleventh Annual World Culture Day a Success.*

World Culture Day was a second-grade event in Foxfield, if you were in Mr. Harley's class.

The article was about a month and a half late, of course, but sometimes the *Biweekly* did that—saved fluffy stories to print weeks later when news was slow. Apparently, Mr. Harley's World Culture Day was still a highlight of the school year.

I looked over the article quickly and sighed, remembering.

I had Mr. Harley in second grade.

So did Vic.

And so did Trina.

If I had just raised my hand for Argentina or Thailand or Mexico, or really any other country at all for the World Culture project, maybe Trina wouldn't hate me so much.

But no—I had to pick South Korea.

My first choice had been China, because the food at Jade Noodle Shop was my absolute favorite, but Nina Moore got China, and I ended up with South Korea.

Trina picked South Korea too, but Mr. Harley assigned her Russia instead.

Korea was an obvious choice for Trina since her older brother, Trey, had been adopted from Korea as a baby. I had no personal connection to Korea at all, so why did I pick it?

I'd have to blame Aunt Julie.

Aunt Julie had just taken my mom and me to a Korean restaurant for the very first time, and we loved everything about it: the wooden tables only ten inches off the ground, the square red pillows inviting us to sit snuggled side by side, the rectangular paper lanterns hanging from the ceiling, giving off a dim and cozy light. The waitresses wore traditional robes as they served us bowl after tiny bowl of precut food to mix in with our rice: vegetables of every texture and color, sauces, mushrooms, dumplings, egg.

The smell and taste of the delicious food were still fresh in my mind and on my tongue when Mr. Harley explained the project we were about to begin, so after I lost out on China, South Korea seemed like a good idea.

We had two weeks to prepare our displays, and I went all out. The day of the event I set up poster board with my own watercolor paintings of snow-covered mountains, wide fields of rice, and rocky land jutting into beautiful blue sea. I made another poster about fermented foods, with an ink drawing of a fermentation pot used to make kimchi, a traditional Korean food. I had paper menus from the Korean restaurant Aunt Julie had taken us to, and a tray of chopsticks people could practice using. I gave chopstick lessons throughout the morning, which I was only able to do because Aunt Julie had drilled me until I mastered the technique. She made me pick up dozens of raisins and drop them in a jar until my hand cramped and the sight of a raisin made my head spin.

But the best part of my display was the food, which Aunt Julie had helped me prepare. I had a vat of warm rice and lots of small dishes containing some of the key elements to *bibim-bap*. *Bibim* means "mixed" and *bap* means "cooked rice," which I explained while visitors made their own bowls of *bibimbap*, choosing from seasoned carrot, cucumber, shitake mushroom, radish, bean sprouts, and a red chili paste sauce to mix into their rice. I also had a regular soy sauce for people who didn't like spicy.

My display was a hit because of the food.

Vic's French table was also really popular because she had cheesy, warm samples of quiche Lorraine cut up on small plates for everyone to try.

Trina didn't have a crowd.

Trina had a pretty set of Russian nesting dolls for people to play with and a whole book of postcards showing Moscow and Saint Petersburg and Russian architecture and landscapes, but the only food she had was borscht.

Borscht is a traditional Russian soup. It was a staple of the Russian diet, especially in the freezing-cold months, when it became the best way to warm up from the inside out. It was also bright red, and superthick, and suspiciously lumpy. It did *not* look appetizing. When Joey Tarquinio left his Guatemala table to look at the other displays and saw the huge bowl of borscht, he yelled, "Eww, blood! I'm not eating blood!"

Mr. Harley had a private talk with Joey then, and one of the teacher's aides told Trina her soup looked delicious, but it was too late.

At the end of the event, as we were starting to clean up, I asked Trina if I could taste her borscht. (Aunt Julie hadn't taken me to a Russian restaurant yet.)

Trina looked at me with a face hard as stone.

"You don't know anything!" she shrieked at me, her eyes

blazing. "You're not even Korean!"

And I saw it—the rage in her.

She should have been mad at Joey for making fun of her soup.

Or at Mr. Harley for assigning her Russia instead of South Korea.

But no, she was mad at me.

I should have folded that day when we both raised our hand for the same country. I should have dropped my arm and let her have it. I should have walked away. But I was only in second grade, and I didn't.

I shuddered at the memory and let out a long, deep breath, hard enough to push it away from me.

I fanned the newsletters out on the counter and read another headline: *Mayor Investigates Need for Library*. The article began: "With technology advances in today's society and universal access to the internet, is a public library an effective and efficient use of taxpayers' money? Mayor Trippley is currently—"

The bell jingled then, and I looked up to see a family walk in with two huge IKEA bags stuffed to the top with books to return. I neatly placed the *Biweekly* on top of the stack and made my way over to Sonia to help.

Shady

>>>·<<<

"It's been three hours, so I'll check the book drops again," I called to Beverly later that day as I walked by her open office door.

"That would be great, Jamie. Thank you," she responded without breaking the pace of her lightning-fast tapping on her keyboard.

I grabbed my water bottle and a library bag for the returned books and headed outside.

The bells clanged behind me as the library door closed and I immediately felt the harsh temperature change from the air-conditioned building to the steamy midday heat. It was so humid out it felt like there was no air in the air.

I walked around the building to the book-drop containers in back, sipping my water slowly, feeling the trickle of cold slide down my throat.

As I approached the two containers, the one for audio materials on the left and the larger one for books on the right, I stopped at the sight of a small brown mound squeezed between the two that hadn't been there at my last visit. It looked like the overused mophead from the library storage closet. As I got closer, it looked more like some old Halloween wig that had been abandoned outside, left to collect dirt and twigs and dust.

But then it moved.

I stepped closer and dropped to my knees, then leaned forward into the small space. And then I knew for sure.

"Hiya, sweetie," I said softly. "It's okay."

A head popped out from under the mound so suddenly I jumped. Two orange-brown eyes peered at me, while a small black nose wiggled frantically as it gathered my scent. I made a loose fist and stretched it in front of the little dog's face so it could get an easy whiff.

"Who are you, little guy?" I asked in a voice about two octaves higher than my regular one. Aunt Julie always said to use a voice that was high-pitched and soft with a new animal, and it seemed to be working. The little dog uncurled itself and stood, did a downward-dog-like yoga stretch, and then padded over to sniff me more completely.

The dog was dirty, and I quickly discovered that it was a he. His fur felt cool to the touch, despite the heat outside.

"You're a smart one, huh? You found some nice shade

between these bins." I ran my hand down his bony back and then scratched lightly under his chin. My hand came away a dark gray, as if I had rubbed the inside of a chimney instead of a sweet little dog. "Cool as a cucumber and super filthy."

He licked my hand. His tongue was dry and rough.

"Oh, sweetie, you need a drink." I quickly uncapped my water bottle.

I poured a bit of water into my hand and he stuck his whole small muzzle right in, lapping up every drop quickly and greedily. I poured more water into my palm, and then more, and he kept drinking. Soon his tongue felt as wet and slick as my palm, which was now dripping with water and dog saliva.

I poured a quickly dissolving ice cube into my hand and placed it in the shade back between the book-drop bins. The dog sauntered back to his shady, quiet spot and settled next to the ice cube. He sniffed it, pawed it, and then proceeded to lick it, delicately trapping it between his two front paws.

"So, no collar. And you look like a hot mess, no offense," I told him. "You all on your own?"

He just looked at me as I spoke, licked his ice cube a few more times, and then sneezed.

"I have to actually do my job now," I told him. As I punched in the code on the audio bin, the dog locked his eyes on me, watching my every move with his head cocked to the side. The ice cube was now down to the size of a green pea on the pavement in front of him. I reached into the drop, pulled out a small stack of DVDs, and then closed the door more gently than usual, trying not to jar the whole metal container and scare the dog. I emptied the book container the same way, stashing the dozen picture books into the library bag alongside the DVDs.

"All right, I have to go back inside now," I told him, reaching my fist in front of his furry head again. He stood and leaned toward it, sniffed and licked me a few more times, then circled once and settled back in his perfect spot of shade. The ice cube was gone. He shut his eyes, sighed once heavily, and resumed his nap.

"I'll bring you water again before I leave. And I'll see if I can find you some food."

I walked the bag of returns back into the library and unloaded them onto the circ desk for Sonia.

A patron walked up at the same time and dropped three books loudly onto the counter in front of Sonia.

"Ready to check out?" Sonia asked politely.

The patron didn't answer, and he didn't even glance at Sonia. He just tossed his card at her and started tapping his fingers against the counter impatiently.

Sonia had explained to me that there were two kinds of people in the world: those who handed you their card and those who counter-dropped it. The patrons who handed you their card were typically pleasant and respectful and polite. They said please and thank you and wished you well as they left. The patrons who dropped their cards didn't bother to wish you a thing. They were usually curt and rude and wouldn't even make eye contact.

Sonia scanned his card and books and neatly packed them into a bag for him. "Thank you very much, sir. Have a lovely day." She smiled widely at him. She had also told me she liked to lay it on extra thick with the card-droppers. "Kill them with kindness," she had said.

The rude guy swung his bag off the counter and quickly left.

"Classic card-dropper?" I asked.

"In the flesh," she confirmed. "What a treat for me."

I laughed. Then I said, "I need to wash my hands," holding them up, fingers spread, as if I were contaminated with hazardous material.

"Yes, some of these books come back pretty funky," Sonia responded.

"No, I was petting a dog, actually. I found a dog out back."

"By the tree? A tall black dog? That's Mrs. Shiu's," Sonia said.

"No, it wasn't tied. It was just there. And it was small. It looked like a stray."

"Ay, go wash up, mami. You don't even know what you were touching." Sonia made a face and backed away from me to make her point.

"All right, I'm going," I laughed, and headed downstairs to the staff kitchen.

I poured a heaping glob of dish soap onto my hands and rubbed until it got foamy. The grime of the dog slid right off under the bubbles of soap. I imagined bringing the dog down to the sink—he would fit in it, no problem—and lathering him up the same way until all the matted dirt was out of his fur and he shone clean and smelled like lemons.

I wondered if I should call a shelter or animal control. The dog could be sick, or infested with some kind of worm or bug. Obviously no one was taking care of him. But what if the shelter decided to put him down because they didn't have enough room for him, or enough money to feed one more animal? Was he better off on his own, the way I found him? I couldn't tell how old he was, but he definitely wasn't a puppy. My mom would kill me if I mentioned the dog to Aunt Julie. She always said Aunt Julie's house was only two tails away from turning into a roadside zoo. My mom would also say the dog knew how to deal and was fine on his own. He *was* smart enough to nap in a safe, shady spot between the two bins, so maybe she was right.

That was a good name, actually: Shady.

I finished rinsing a second round of soap off my hands and wrists and dried myself on a paper towel that was rough as bark, absorbing pretty much no water at all, exactly like the sad paper towels at the middle school. I dried my hands the rest of the way on my shorts and climbed the steps back to the main floor of the library.

Sonia

→≫·≪←

"What a surprise!" Sonia greeted me as I walked through the library door on Friday morning. I had already met my hours for the week, so I bet she wasn't expecting me to come in today.

"And look at you—wicked side braid." She smiled at me and raised her eyebrows.

"I didn't have anything else to do today, so . . ." I tried to say it so it wouldn't sound as pathetic as it was. A thirteen-year-old girl on summer vacation with nothing better to do than volunteer extra hours at her public library? I had hit an all-time low.

"Good timing, then, because there's *lots* to do in the children's room today," Sonia said. "We had day camp visitors, *preschool* age."

"That's cool," I replied.

"Cool? Oh, Jamie, you have no idea." She shook her head at me.

"It's cool that they would bring them here, to a library, I mean. That's a good field trip," I explained.

"Yes, a great field trip. But I have never seen so many runny noses in my life. And it's summer! That's not supposed to happen in summertime, right?" She ducked under the desk and then popped back up with two containers of sani-wipes, one in each hand. "Pretty much every inch of the room needs a wipe-down."

"Oh, it's not so bad, Sonia." Lenny appeared out of the back room, laughing and rolling an empty cart back to the circ desk. "All those germs make your immunity stronger."

"I've worked here forever. My immunity is iron-plated," Sonia bragged. "I still like my library clean."

Lenny laughed again and took the containers from her hands. "I'll take care of it."

"I'd start with the puzzles," Sonia added, "and the blocks table. I'll do the touch screens myself with the special wipes."

"Whatever you say, boss." Lenny bowed at her, then stopped short as he read the label on one of the containers she'd handed him. "Jeez, Sonia, you gave me the hard stuff. This'll peel paint off the walls."

"Then my professional advice is," Sonia said, as she scrolled a new roll of receipt tape into the printer, "do not use them on the walls."

"Very funny," Lenny said, then headed toward the employee staircase. "I'm putting rubber gloves on before I reach into this vessel of toxic cleanser."

"*Disinfecting* toxic cleanser!" Sonia said, a little too loud for a library.

"I'll risk the chemical exposure," Lenny said to Sonia as he disappeared downstairs, "but only for you."

I raised my eyebrows at Sonia.

"Don't look at me like that," she warned, purposely not making eye contact with me. "Lenny's a nice guy. He's like that with everyone."

"If you say so." I smirked back.

"So Lenny's dealing with the children's toys"—Sonia ignored me—"which means we'll put you to work here. You can help with returns. I'm going to scan in this pile"—she gestured to three tall stacks of books and DVDs on the counter to her left—"and then hand them to you to scan again. Every item should be double-checked before it gets shelved."

"Okay," I said, excited to finally get to use a circulation computer.

"Here's the inventory check screen. Just run the bar code

under here"—she demonstrated, and the scanner let out a high-pitched *beep*—"and then pile them on the cart behind you here."

"Got it."

"You have to look at the screen, though, to see each title register. Sometimes it beeps but it doesn't scan, so you have to see it on the screen with your eyes."

"Okay."

"And take your time. You don't have to go as fast as me."

"Okay."

"Better to be slow and accurate."

"Okay."

"I think I should buy you a special coffee mug that says 'Okay' on it," Sonia teased me.

"Okay," I teased her back.

And then the bell jingled and a man in a bright blue tie entered the library and walked straight up to Sonia.

"Good morning. How are you today?" he asked.

"Fine, thank you. How can I help you?" she replied, putting down the book she was holding and giving her full attention to him.

"I'm here to see Beverly Cooper. I'm Edward Trippley."

"Oh." Sonia looked skeptical. "I didn't realize she had a meeting this morning."

"Oh, she's not expecting me. I just wanted to have a face-to-face." He straightened his tie then and unbuttoned his suit jacket. "I started as mayor earlier this year, as you may know, and I'm here to talk about how to best serve our wonderful town of Foxfield."

"Of course," Sonia said, looking more doubtful still but putting on her best welcoming smile. "I'm Sonia, and this is our volunteer, Jamie. We both live here in town." Sonia reached across the counter and shook Mayor Trippley's hand.

He shook her hand back, and then shook mine as well. "Very nice to meet you, of course." It felt like his glance lingered on me for an extra moment, like maybe he was trying to remember something he might have heard about a student "working" at the library. My palms started to itch, and I rubbed them against the sides of my shorts the way Beverly rubbed her hands against her corduroys.

"I'll just phone Beverly, in her office, to let her know you're here."

"Don't go to any trouble. I'll just head on back myself. Just a friendly visit." And with that he excused himself, quickly finding his way back to Beverly's office, Sonia still holding the phone to her ear.

She dialed anyway. "Maybe she'll pick up before he reaches the door," she whispered to me. And then quietly, to herself,

"She deserves a little warning."

The phone rang and rang, and then we heard a door open and close. "He got to her first." Sonia bit her lip in frustration and hung up the phone.

Lenny came out of the children's room, his hands in bright yellow gloves. "Was that the new mayor?"

I nodded yes.

A thoughtful "hmm" came from Lenny as he stared at the closed door. Then he looked over to Sonia.

"What do you think?" he asked her.

"I think he's getting the wrong idea, coming now when we're empty. Most of the day we're so busy with patrons," she said, as if Lenny didn't already know this. "And I think I'm not feeling the *friendly* in that friendly visit."

Lenny thought for a moment, then said, "Let's not jump to conclusions. You never know."

"What's going on?" I asked, completely baffled.

"Nothing, Jamie," Lenny answered me before Sonia could. "So far, nothing's going on." And then his voice got louder as he declared, "It's just another beautiful morning in the library." He raised his long arms out to the sides, one yellow-sheathed hand still holding a canister of sani-wipes, and beamed a broad, goofy smile, turning in a circle like Moses on top of a mountain.

Sonia laughed and her shoulders relaxed. "What would

we do without you, Lenny?"

And Lenny beamed even more.

An hour later Mayor Trippley walked out of Beverly's office. He lifted his hand at me like he was waving from a parade float and walked briskly out of the library.

Beverly stepped out of her office a minute later. Her eyes were glazed and her cheeks were flushed. She looked smaller, like a balloon that had lost some of its air.

Lenny froze at the circ desk, his mouth open like he was about to say something but then changed his mind. Sonia emerged from the staff stairway at the exact moment that Beverly cleared her throat, brushed her hands down the sides of her pants, and then cleared her throat again, more forcefully this time.

She looked down at the floor and then back up. "We have a problem," she said.

All I heard after that was the crack of Sonia's coffee mug hitting the floor.

I cleaned up the spilled coffee while Lenny, Sonia, and Beverly all sat down in Beverly's office. They closed the door, so I was alone, just me and a handful of patrons.

I straightened my posture behind the circ desk and tucked my hair behind my ears. I scanned the room and noticed some magazines left behind on a chair. I stacked them in order and returned them to their shelf, then pushed in a chair at a computer desk so it wouldn't block the aisle.

When a man on a computer looked up at me, I smiled and nodded at him, the same way Beverly would.

A woman in a suit and heels strolled into the library with a pile of books.

"Are those returns? I can take them for you," I offered.

"Thank you very much," she said, and then strolled right back out.

An older man came down the staircase from the loft and made a beeline for me. "Excuse me, miss. Do you have travel books?"

"We do. Right this way." I walked him to the travel section, in the 900s. I knew exactly where they were because I had spent a half hour shelf-reading that section the other day.

On my way back to the circ desk, I caught my reflection on a dark computer screen that had gone to sleep. At first I didn't recognize myself, because the person in the reflection looked happy. The person in the reflection looked like someone who belonged exactly where they were.

A pang of guilt shot through me when I remembered how I'd felt just a few weeks ago: that it would be great if the library closed and I didn't have to work here.

Suddenly, that was the absolute last thing I wanted.

Trina

❯❯❯·❮❮❮

We were always swamped with returns on Mondays, since we were closed all weekend long in the summer months. It took me four trips just to empty the book drop, and almost an hour to get the books put away.

After that was done, I watched the circ desk while Sonia hunted for printer ink in the supply closet downstairs and Beverly helped a patron on a computer. Lenny wouldn't be in for another hour.

I took a long sip of water from the bottle I kept over the money drawer, right next to Sonia's coffee mug. I was mid-swallow when the bells on the front door jangled like a cymbal crashing to the ground. I looked up from the circ desk and found myself face-to-face with Trina.

My stomach did a complete flip and landed on itself, hard

and flat and without mercy, like a belly flop at a very crowded public pool.

The heat began its creep up my neck. I wished I could stop it, that red flush, before it got to my cheeks and broadcast my humiliation. I thought of Sonia. Poised, professional, knowledgeable Sonia, who treated every patron equally and respectfully, no matter who they were. Sonia, who just *had* to leave the circ desk about ten seconds before Trina walked in.

I channeled the power of Sonia and forced out the only four words I could think of: "Can I help you?"

I could *not* muster a Sonia smile, though.

I watched as Trina's eyes went to the top of my head. She was checking out my hair, the inverted French braid my mom had styled for me before leaving for work this morning. I still couldn't manage this kind of braid myself, so occasionally I would sit on the coffee table in front of the TV, watching whatever awful talk show was on at that hour while my mom worked her hairstyling magic on me. I handed her comb, brush, hair ties at her command, like a nurse handing over a scalpel, swab, clamp in surgery. That had been our routine since I was little. I always sat right in that same spot on the corner of the low table while she did my hair for the day. Having the TV on kept me still and cooperative when I was little, but now it was just part of our tradition.

Earlier that morning, we couldn't find anything decent to watch.

"An entire morning segment on the correct length of capris for your leg type?" my mom managed to say around the hairband she held clenched between her teeth.

"Well, thank God we know," I answered, giggling at how dumb it was.

"These shows are getting worse by the day," my mom exclaimed. "They are ruining us as a people."

"They are ruining us as a country!" I continued. "As capris-wearing citizens!"

"It's a travesty," my mom decided.

"Should I turn it off?" I offered.

"God no! It's so bad it's almost good." And she continued braiding while we watched the next segment, which explained how to decorate a summer patio in a country-rustic style.

I saw Trina's eyes follow the curve of my braid all the way to the end. She was probably disappointed that it looked too good to make fun of later when she saw her posse. I was instantly grateful that I had started to make the effort to come to the library not looking like I had just rolled out of bed.

"I'm returning these," Trina said, staring me right in the eyes. She dropped two cookbooks on the counter in front of me. "We had an amazing party over the weekend. Everyone said my food was awesome."

Wow, Trina sure was comfortable bragging about herself. It must be nice to have that much self-confidence.

I managed to say "Thank you" the same way Sonia did when she took returns from patrons. I turned away, thinking it would be a great time to take a break downstairs in the staff kitchen where I could recover, but Trina called me back.

"And I need something else, too," she said, eyes sparkling. Her blue eyes were unfairly pretty. "I'm looking for a book. You probably know it, by Charlotte Brontë. It's called *Jane Eyre*."

Trina didn't so much as blink; I bet she didn't want to risk missing even a second of my suffering. I felt my cheeks burn a hot red. I was speechless, frozen in my spot, like a deer in headlights.

And then I felt a hand on my shoulder, a warm touch.

"I can show you where the novels are. Please follow me." Sonia turned before Trina could respond and walked toward the staircase that led to the loft.

Trina narrowed her eyes at me and then followed Sonia, even though we both knew she didn't actually need that book.

I made a break for it downstairs, found a chair, and lowered my shaky self into it. I crossed my arms on the tabletop, dropped my heavy head on top of them, and cried.

Beverly

-»»·«««-

"Is there anything I can do, Jamie?"

Beverly's voice was quiet and careful.

"I'm sorry," I said, lifting my head slowly. "I'm okay."

The genuine look of concern on Beverly's face made me want to start crying all over again.

"Sonia told me you were down here," Beverly admitted. "I just wanted to check on you."

"Thanks," I managed to say.

"Here." She took a box of tissues off the shelf and, after looking at my face again, handed the whole box to me. I must have looked frightening.

"Thanks," I said again. I cleaned up my face, blew my nose, and balled up the tissues in my pitiful, sorry fists.

"So, *Jane Eyre*," Beverly said, pulling out the chair beside me and lowering herself into it. "That's on the eighth-grade curriculum?"

"Yeah," I answered, instead of saying *yes*, which I had been trying to say instead. Sonia never answered questions with *yeah*. "It's the final exam," I added.

"Oh dear." She let out a sigh. "The final."

I let out a sigh, too, then explained, "You read it with the class, but the final exam is a bunch of essay questions you have to answer in that blue test booklet in school."

She let out a short huff. "The perfect way to kill a classic."

My eyes scrunched up. "What?"

"It's a wonderful book. One of my favorites," she revealed. "But it never would have been if I had to study it inside and out for a middle school exam. That's how you kill a book for students. It's a shame."

Beverly clasped her locket and slid it back and forth on the chain around her neck for a moment as she thought. "There has to be a way to use the classics in school without destroying the beauty of them."

She looked truly distraught over this.

"Well, we read *Alice's Adventures in Wonderland* this year, in seventh grade," I offered, still dabbing at my nose with a tissue. "And we had a big test on it, but I still liked it by the end of the unit."

"Well, that's good to hear." Beverly nodded, looking somewhat relieved.

"But . . . that might be because I'd read it outside of school, so I already had my own opinion about it." I sat up a little straighter and felt my stomach begin to settle back in its place. I took a long, deep breath and let it out slowly.

"Alice is so charming," Beverly said, then recited from memory, "'I almost wish I hadn't gone down that rabbit hole—and yet, and yet—it's rather curious, you know, this sort of life.'"

I smiled. "Curiouser and curiouser," I said.

Beverly smiled back at me, then looked me right in the eyes, her face serious, and asked, "Have you read *Jane Eyre* yet? On your own?"

"Yes."

"Really?" she asked, surprised.

"Well, I watched the movie first with my mom, and I loved it, so then she borrowed the book from her friend at work and we read it last summer."

"How lovely."

"It's a hard book, though. Some of the language—we had to read it together so I'd understand it."

"And?"

"And I loved it. So much. Jane is incredible, what she overcomes, how she faces every day, and then Mr. Rochester, how she is with him. I was blown away by her. But now I . . . It just reminds me—" I couldn't finish the sentence.

"No," Beverly commanded. Her face was stern and she was pointing at me. "Do *not* let what happened at school ruin the book for you. That would be like rewriting the ending of a book because it didn't please you, and you can't do that. Endings aren't there to please you. Endings happen the way they do for a reason. Do you understand, Jamie? This is important." She softened her voice a bit then and folded her hands in her lap.

"Yes," I said, returning her gaze.

"Don't rewrite your feelings for that book. *Jane Eyre* is remarkable. It was, and it still is."

"Okay," I promised. "It still is."

"You cannot rewrite your own past, either. It's a tremendous waste of energy to cling so tightly to things you cannot undo."

Beverly's gaze moved from my face then to some empty space between us, her eyes glazing over slightly. Then, as if reading right from a book, she recited, "'Life appears to me too short to be spent in nursing animosity or registering wrongs.'"

I watched her, waiting for her to explain.

When she didn't, I asked, "Is that from the chair upstairs?"

"It's from *Jane Eyre*." Beverly pulled herself out of her trance, clasped her necklace gently, and then let it go. "Helen Burns said it."

"Oh, Helen!" I remembered right away. "That was the

saddest part for me. I hated that, when she died. It was so unfair."

Beverly's head moved up and down the tiniest bit in acknowledgment.

"It was like Jane lost the only real friend she'd ever had," I said. I was so angry at Charlotte Brontë for making Helen die that I started to write her a letter, but my mom told me it was a wasted effort, since the author died in 1855.

I was still mad about it, though. "It felt like Jane lost a sister when Helen died," I explained to Beverly.

Beverly blinked several times in a row, as if something had suddenly landed in her eye and she was working to set it free. Then she folded her hands together on the tabletop and said, "Jane lost her, yes, but she also found a way to keep Helen with her always, in her words, in the example of the life she led."

I thought about that for a minute. Helen was gone, and having the memory of her was not the same as having the actual person. It couldn't be. But I didn't say that to Beverly. She seemed to be having her own moment, lost in thoughts pulled from the attic of her mind. I wasn't at all sure how we got from eighth-grade finals to the subject of death, but I *had* recovered from the Trina incident upstairs.

"You look like you're feeling better," Beverly said then, as if reading my mind.

"Yeah. I mean, yes." I straightened my posture in my chair. "I am."

"Okay, then. Well," Beverly stood and neatly pushed in her chair. She returned the box of tissues to the shelf and nodded at me.

"Thank you, Beverly." Those two little words didn't seem like nearly enough for how grateful I felt to her.

"You're very welcome." She smiled, then turned to leave.

"Wait, Beverly." I stopped her. "What's going to happen to the library? Are we getting shut down?"

Beverly took a deep breath and let it out slowly. "It seems that's what the mayor wants, yes. He intends to close us, to address town budget issues."

"He can't do that! We can't let him."

"We don't intend to, but it's complicated. Our annual cost to the town isn't that high. The problem is this building. It needs so many repairs—it would cost the town a fortune to cover them. The mayor thinks it's easier to shut us down completely than fix the building. But we're working on a plan. Lenny is already drafting a petition to show that residents value the library."

"If there's anything I can do to help, I'd like to."

Beverly smiled wide and said, "That's wonderful, Jamie. I'm so happy to hear the library matters to you so much."

It was true. The library mattered to me.

Then she said, "Take a moment to get yourself together and then come back upstairs. There's lots to do."

After Beverly left, I stood up, stretched my arms up to the water-damaged basement ceiling, and checked my reflection in the mirror. I splashed cold water on my face, gave my cheeks a few pinches, and climbed the stairs to the main floor.

Trina was long gone by the time I got back to the circ desk, and the afternoon was slow. I had time to look through the art books in the 700s and picked out one on Georgia O'Keeffe and one on Vincent van Gogh to take home with me. I also had time to make a pencil sketch of Wally's Tuesday flower and another drawing of the old woodwork details that decorated the fireplace mantel in the reading room. I was about to try a quick sketch of Black Hat Guy, who was sound asleep in his quotes chair, but then he popped awake the second I put my first mark on the paper. He headed to the bathroom and I decided to go home. It was almost five o'clock and I was starving. The sandwich I'd packed for lunch was like a distant memory, and there were no Lenny treats in the staff room to sample.

I rounded the library to cut through the parking lot in back, passing the book drop containers on my left as I went. I looked for the dog between them, but he wasn't there. What was there, though, was some kind of small bowl. I walked closer to get a better look and saw what looked to be a to-go coffee cup, ripped down so the sides were only a few inches tall all the way around. It made a decent water bowl, and it had been recently filled, clear, clean water waiting like a still pond for the little dog to lap up.

Maybe I wasn't the only one looking out for Shady.

Wally

->>>·<<<-

Wally had sweated two big rings of damp under each of his arms by the time he made it to me at the circulation desk on Tuesday morning. He pulled a handkerchief out of his pocket—a real handkerchief, like you see in old-time movies—and blotted his forehead and neck.

"Good morning to you, and a good morning it is." Wally panted out his greeting.

"It's a rough one out there today, isn't it, Wally?" Lenny asked him, pushing a cart of new books over to the display wall.

"Yes, sirree," Wally replied, lowering his handkerchief and looking at the smears of wet grime on it. "This summer is too hot for me, I tell ya."

"I'll second that. I got up at four in the morning today to get started on a paint job, just to beat the heat. The paint was practically boiling in the can the other day when I was working at noon."

Wally cracked a broad smile and chuckled. "Boiling in the can. Is that right?"

"Practically," Lenny answered him. "You can feel the AC best in that corner back there." He motioned to the children's room behind him. "Why don't you rest there for a little while, cool yourself off a bit?"

"I just might do that," Wally answered him. "I just might. Thank you very much."

Wally folded his handkerchief tidily and then slipped it back into his shirt pocket. He pulled a white carnation out of his plastic grocery bag, which was more torn and mangy-looking than it was last Tuesday, something I hadn't thought possible. He really seemed to take that Reduce, Reuse, Recycle thing seriously, except he seemed to be permanently stuck on *Reuse*. I bet he had drawers full of used rubber bands at home and cabinets overflowing with empty glass jars, their lids impossible to find because they were all stuffed into another bursting plastic bag somewhere.

"There you go," Wally said to his flower as he placed it in the vase and removed the old one. "Pretty as a picture."

"Hi, Wally," I greeted him. "Thank you for the new flower."

"Oh, you're always welcome for the flowers. I bring my

flicks and I bring my flowers," Wally said, gesturing to the movies still banded together in his bag. Then he started coughing, barely getting his arm up in time to cover his mouth. His whole body lurched forward on the last deep cough of the set. It was so loud and full it seemed to shake the entire building. He might have even scared himself with that last one—his eyes looked wide with surprise and a trace of fear. He lowered his arm from his mouth with a slight tremor, then shook his head.

"That was a whopper," he said, to himself or to me, I wasn't sure. One thing was sure, though, and that was that every single person in the library was staring at him. It was *that* loud.

Beverly came out of her office and clasped her hands in front of her chest, looking at Wally with worry lines etched across her forehead, deep as rake marks in sand.

Lenny caught Beverly's eye and nodded to let her know he was on it.

He approached Wally, concern shading his face. He put his hand on Wally's shoulder, and his voice went soft. "Been to a doctor about that cough yet, young man?"

That was so like Lenny, to call him *young man*. I didn't know for sure, but it looked like Wally was at least eighty years old.

"Ehh." Wally waved him off. "No need for a doctor."

"You've sounded better, Wally," Lenny told him gently, "at least to these ears."

"I've sounded like this as long as I've known me," Wally joked. "Don't need to see a doc for a plain old cough."

"Just a plain old cough, Wally?" Lenny asked in a tender voice.

Wally's face clouded over for a short, dark moment, then quickly reset itself. I had never seen Wally look anything but content: giddy over his flowers or pleased over his movie selections or happily focused on the wall of brand-new releases. Those were the three phases of Wally I'd seen all summer long.

"A little cough never hurt anyone," Wally told Lenny. "It's good for the insides. Gets everything up and moving around."

Lenny paused a moment, then responded with, "Well, my friend, I have to say that is certainly an interesting way of looking at it." He looked over Wally's head to make eye contact with me and raised his eyebrows.

I shrugged in response. At least Lenny was trying.

"Jamie," Wally addressed me. "I got my DVDs to return."

"Of course, Wally. I'll take those for you." I moved quickly to him so he wouldn't have to release his hold on the counter, which seemed to be keeping him upright.

"This was a really neat one. About an artist who does all these paintings but then her husband takes all the credit for it. True story. Really a good one."

"Really?" I asked, turning the case over in my hands to read the back. It was PG-13, so my mom wouldn't have a problem with me watching it. It was the middle of July and we were way overdue, my mom and Aunt Julie and me, for a movie night together. I missed snuggling up on the couch between them with our traditional movie snacks: root beer and chocolate chip morsels poured right onto hot popcorn so they melted streaks of chocolaty goodness all over the salty kernels. The only thing that would make movie night better would be if Vic were there, too.

The summary on the DVD case explained that the story was about two artists who meet in the park one day, begin to paint together, then fall in love and get married.

Of course, after reading that, my mind jumped right to Art Club.

And Trey.

Art Club met every other Friday after school, from October through June, and was open to all sixth, seventh, and eighth graders. We met in the art room with Mrs. Holm at three o'clock and ate snacks while she lectured us on an artist or a particular style or a new material she wanted us to try. She always had slides to go with her talk, and also books and postcards of prints to pass around. While Trey watched the slides, I snuck glances at him. He was always there early and took the same seat, right up front.

After the slide show, we each worked on our own project

while Mrs. Holm circled around and helped whoever wanted help. I loved those Friday afternoons.

Toward the end of one meeting back in March, a bunch of kids suddenly gathered around Trey, who was busily working with charcoal pencil.

"Oh my God, man. That is amazing," Michael, a seventh grader, said loud enough for the whole room to hear.

"That is so unfair," Olivia, an eighth grader, chimed in, leaning over his shoulder to get a closer look. "Can I take a picture of that?" She snapped a shot with her phone before he could even answer.

More kids left what they were working on to see Trey's drawing.

"Whoa, Trey. That's sick," another eighth grader told him.

Trey smiled and thanked each person who complimented him, but you could tell he was in the zone and didn't want to stop drawing long enough for a conversation.

A few more kids walked over to see his work and I went with them, swarming with the crowd for a peek. More compliments rang out and one boy even said, "Okay, I'll have to burn mine now. It cannot live in a world where that drawing lives." He got a few laughs, but Trey didn't respond. He just kept moving his hand over his paper, sketching lines here and there, adding depth with crosshatching and shading.

Before I knew it, I was the only one left still looking, standing next to Trey with my mouth slightly open, staring at his work. My eyes kept fighting over drinking in his drawing, which was of an old rowboat washed ashore with a seagull in flight above it, or his hands, which were smooth and graceful and captivating in the way they made the charcoal glide over the paper.

He paused and leaned back in his chair, relaxing for a moment, and then looked up at me. "Hey, Jamie."

"Hi," I said back, my heart pounding in my ears.

"How's yours coming?" he asked, when I continued to just stand and stare at him.

"What? Mine?" I stumbled. "It's okay."

"Can I see?" he asked.

"No. I mean, yes. It's just, it's not that good, not like yours," I admitted.

He followed me to my easel.

"I don't know. I'll probably just start it over." I tilted my head as I looked at my drawing, searching for something good in it.

Trey studied it for a bit and then said, "I like this part here, where these two lines meet." He ran his hand over the bottom of the page, where the edge of a vase met the rounded side of a pepper grinder. I was drawing from a still life Mrs. Holm had set up for me.

"I like the shading you did, too," he said. "That looks pretty cool."

I looked at it and tried to see what he saw. With his hand in front of it, pointing, it suddenly looked cool to me, too. "Thanks," I managed to say. And then I wanted to say his name. "Trey. Thanks a lot."

He smiled and shrugged, then walked back to his easel.

I couldn't understand how Trey and Trina could be siblings. Trey was as soft-spoken and modest and genuinely nice as any eighth-grade boy could possibly be, while Trina was loud and attention-hungry and brash in every move she made.

Vic had her own goofy theory to explain it: "Trina clearly swallows a whopping handful of mean-girl pills each morning with her no-pulp orange juice. Maybe she'll run out some day and become human again. Maybe she won't. But Trey—he doesn't even know *how* to be mean. He's just a really decent person. He can't help it."

I totally agreed with her there. I had seen him leave his easel in a snap to help other kids who were struggling with a drawing, and I'd also seen him stay after Art Club on Fridays when everyone else took off so he could help Mrs. Holm wash the tables and organize supplies.

Trey was better than decent. Trey was the guy who would give you half his sandwich without a second thought after Eddie Gazerro knocked your entire lunch tray to the floor.

Trey was the guy who looked the crossing guard right in the eye and said thank you every single morning when she stopped traffic so we could cross the street to get to school.

Or this told it best, how beyond decent Trey was: When Cassidy Carter showed up at school with scabs and scratches all over the right side of her face in sixth grade and kids bombarded her all day with, "Oh my God!" and "What happened to your face?" Trey was the one person who simply asked her, "Cassidy, are you okay?" It honestly made *me* want to be the one who fell off my bike and came to school covered in gross scabs and peeling skin.

How could you not fall completely head over heels for a guy like that? Who was so wonderfully kind. Who could also draw. And who was also cuter then cute.

I was in deep.

I never missed an Art Club Friday the entire school year. Until the end of May. Part of my *consequences* was that I couldn't attend my club. I missed the end-of-year show, where the best of our work was displayed in the auditorium like an actual gallery opening, with author tags taped to the wall under our pieces and lace-covered tables of crackers and cookies set out for refreshments. Trey never missed Art Club either, except for once. He wasn't at Art Club the day after Trina posted my letter. He didn't even come to school that day. To know that something I wrote embarrassed him *that* much hurt like crazy. It hurt probably just as much as a bad husband taking credit for his wife's artwork, like in that movie Wally just returned.

Wally would spend a solid half hour now poring over the DVD collection, sliding out cases to inspect the front cover, read the description on the back, and then flip back to the cover again. Sometimes he even pulled up a chair. It bothered Beverly because the chair blocked the aisle and made it difficult for other patrons to get around, but she let him do it anyway. Because it was Wally.

"Thanks for the movie recommendation, Wally," I called to him. "I think I'll take it home."

"Oh, you're welcome, dear. It's a good one. All about art. Love and art," he called to me from his perch.

"Love and art," I repeated under my breath, but I guess I was louder than I thought, because Wally responded to me.

"Yep, a great combination," he said, "love and art." He cleared his throat, then added, "Until it's not."

He laughed then, deep and guttural, and then starting coughing into his fist.

Lenny

→≫·≪←

"**L**et me help you with that, Jamie."

Lenny was already in the staff kitchen when I came down with two big boxes of supplies that had just arrived. Deliveries always came on Monday afternoons. I had been spending so much time at the library that I now knew this kind of information. Sonia even let me sign for the delivery today, which made me feel like a pretty big deal.

Lenny took both boxes out of my hands in one swoop.

"Thanks. Beverly said there's a closet down here for all this stuff?" I asked.

"There is, right here." He slid a half-full file cabinet a few inches to the left and then swung open a partially concealed door. The door was peeling paint in long strips and the doorknob didn't turn. Lenny had to just pull it, really hard, to get the door open. "We're a little pressed for space here, and maintenance funds, if you hadn't noticed."

"Oh, I noticed," I told him.

"They don't build 'em like this anymore, though." Lenny looked up at the ceiling above us and spun in place, slowly. "I mean, look at the detail in the woodwork on this door. And look at this doorknob. You can't buy these anymore. We even have a dumbwaiter! No one has a dumbwaiter!"

"There's a dumbwaiter here? Like in *Harriet the Spy*?" I asked.

"Absolutely. On the other side of the stairs you just came down. It still works. It's a bear to pull up and down, but if you've got the muscles, it works."

"That is too cool!"

"I'll show you when we go back up. Sonia showed it to me when I first started here. She knows all the secrets of this place." Lenny's voice got all sweet-sounding when he mentioned Sonia.

"She does, huh?" I couldn't keep the smirk off my face.

Lenny's cheeks flushed a rosy pink that matched the new spatters of pink paint on his shoes.

"Wait, how long have you even been here with us? Three weeks?"

"This is my *sixth* week," I answered in a huff, throwing my hands on my hips dramatically.

"Really?" Lenny asked, surprised.

"I started right after school let out."

I remembered my first day well. I was on the front steps that Monday morning way before the library opened, my stomach squeezing my nerves from the inside out. I had packed my sketchbook to draw in until the doors opened, but I was way too nervous to focus on it. I just wanted to put in my hours and get back home, where I could climb into my bed and hide and pretend this wasn't happening to me.

Maybe if I knew back then that I'd be working with people like Lenny and Sonia and Beverly, I wouldn't have been so nervous.

"Six weeks, huh?" Lenny was still trying to absorb it.

"I've been here long enough to notice that Sonia knows all the secrets around here and that you notice everything Sonia knows, let's just put it that way," I said.

Lenny looked at me and smiled. "Fair enough."

"Sonia's great," I told him.

"Yeah, she is great." He sighed.

He tucked the boxes into the closet and closed the door on them. "I'll organize that later. That's an hour's job at least." He shimmied the file cabinet back in place. "So, are you hungry? You gotta try these," he said, before waiting for my answer.

"They're my newest masterpiece." He gestured to the rickety table behind me. In the middle of it sat a square plate piled high with some kind of unrecognizable food.

"What is it?" I asked, trying to hide my confusion.

"They're cookies, of course." The smile vanished from his face like a drop of water on a hot skillet. He furrowed his brow. "Why? What did you think they were?"

"Cookies," I said unconvincingly.

"No. Really. What did you think they were?" he tried again.

"Um," I shifted my weight, stalling.

"Tell me," he insisted.

"They look like nests."

"Birds' nests?" He was incredulous.

"Really small ones, but yeah, that's what they look like."

"Nests? On a plate?"

I shrugged as apologetically as I could. "That's why I was confused."

"Will everyone think that?" I bet he was really just asking about Sonia, if Sonia would think that.

"I don't know. Are they good? What's in them?"

Lenny proceeded to list the ingredients, which included a lot of different seeds and nuts and nut flours and dried fruits and some things I'd never even heard of. But he definitely said chocolate, and I'm always a big supporter of chocolate, even if it's mixed in with a whole lot of strange healthy stuff.

I tried one. It was sweet and salty and crunchy and chewy all at the same time. And the chocolate was there, like an old friend.

"Lenny, these are actually good."

Lenny smiled big and then got serious again very quickly.

"So you think Sonia will like them?"

"I don't know. I don't know what she likes to eat. I only ever see her drink gallons of coffee." I thought for a second, then offered, "I have an idea! I could give her one to try, and if she loves it, I'll tell her you made it and send her down here to get more. If she doesn't like it, I'll just say I got them from that bakery in town."

"Brilliant. Let's do it." His smile returned. And then he went from normal to supremely overexcited in half a second flat. "Move it then, kiddo. Up you go, right now. Take her this one."

Lenny handed me a cookie on a bright pink napkin. Then he took it back. "Should we put two on here? How about like this? Does this look better?" He was arranging cookies on the napkin as if he were assembling a bride's bouquet.

I couldn't help laughing. "Oh my God, Lenny, you're a little bit flipping out. It's just a cookie." Even though he was an adult, and a gigantic adult at that, it was easy to feel really comfortable around him. Being with him was a lot like hanging out with an older, smarter, really cool friend. It was easy to forget he was older than my own mom.

"If you really wanted to win Sonia over, you would brew her a whole pot of coffee," I told him.

"Way ahead of you there, darling," Lenny answered back with a smirk of his own. And right that second, as if on cue, the Mr. Coffee machine on the counter behind him let out a hiss, and a stream of fresh, hot coffee trickled its way into the glass pot waiting below.

Black Hat Guy

⟫⟫⟫·⟪⟪⟪

The next day, at 4:18, there was no sign of Black Hat Guy. I felt like filing a missing person's report. His chair looked wrong, almost sad, to be empty at this time of day.

Maybe he lost track of time. Maybe he was hanging out at the Bean Pot today instead. Or maybe he got a job. I had overheard him telling Lenny that he was out of work, that he was desperate to find a job somewhere. Anywhere.

A spear of sunlight beamed through the window, highlighting part of a quote on the chair: *tread on my dreams.*

Those four words echoed inside my brain, taunting me, because *tread* sounded like *Trey*, and Trey was my dream. That didn't come true.

Hadn't I dreamt it, how it would all play out so perfectly, in that quick instant that the book opened in my hands and revealed the treasures inside?

Back in May, cocooned between two stacks in the middle school library, hadn't I just planned to check out a copy of *Jane Eyre* to read after watching the movie for the third time? Hadn't I selected the only copy left on the shelf, worn and tattered, the front cover falling open gently in my hand? Hadn't my intentions been good? But then the notes, all those answers, scattered across the end pages and chapter breaks and margins: questions printed, page numbers circled, quotes underlined, essay points outlined, all in super-neat handwriting. Probably all the answers to the eighth-grade language arts final right there, pulsing like a heartbeat, prodding, pushing me to action.

It all played out like a movie in my mind, like a dream: anonymously delivering the book to Trey, Trey acing his exam, Trey puzzling over his book fairy's identity, Trey piecing together clues, and then that time-stopping moment when Trey figured out it was me. Next, my phone ringing, or a text buzzing, or maybe even a knock at my door after running through town to get to me, to thank me, to profess the feelings he didn't know until that moment he had for me.

God, it sounded so stupid now.

It sounded ridiculous.

Because it was ridiculous.

Because Trey would never cheat. He would *never* have used the book with all its easy-access answers. He wasn't that kind of player—that's the one thing I knew about him for sure.

And it was ridiculous because the whole idea was a stupid riot of *movie* romance, which, my mom had taught me, was nothing like *real-life* romance. But I didn't think about that in the moment.

I didn't think at all.

I didn't think about turning the book in.

I didn't think about the Honor Code.

I didn't think about who I was and what I knew was right.

I didn't think about tucking my feelings for Trey down deep into my back pocket long enough to clear my head.

I didn't think about anything except how much I liked Trey.

I hurried out of the library, cradling the book under my sweatshirt, and left the building through the first door I saw. I circled to the playground in back, where kids hung out after school, where backpacks were lined up against the brick wall. I spotted Trey's immediately. It was shiny black, clean, standing perfectly upright, every pocket zipped closed. It had that one patch on the arm strap, that patch I read to myself at every Art Club Friday: *Creativity is allowing yourself to make mistakes. Art is knowing which ones to keep.* It was thoughtful, and original, and deep. Like Trey.

I walked right up to his backpack like it was my own, unzipped the largest compartment, dropped the book in, zipped it back up, and turned to leave. I stutter-stepped to save myself from a fall over a mound of backpacks and gym bags, and when I looked up I saw Trina, her eyes locked onto me. I lost my footing for a second, almost falling again, but saved myself, threw my shoulders back, and quickly walked away.

Maybe she didn't see. Maybe she didn't see. That was the chant that matched my footsteps as I hurried home. Maybe she didn't.

Tread softly because you tread on my dreams. That was the whole quote on the library chair.

Trey was my dream, and Trina was the big iron boot that trod on it. Hard.

Because she did see.

Of course she did.

And of course she went to the principal to turn the book in, to turn *me* in.

It all unfolded painfully after that, like the stickiest Band-Aid in the universe peeled away one tiny decimeter at a time.

On a stage.

Under a spotlight.

For everyone to see.

There had been a strange buzz in the air the next morning at school, an energy that was different from normal. On my way to the lunchroom, I passed a group of girls clustered by the first-floor bathroom, Izzy among them, whispering and gesturing furiously. I hurried past them and beat Vic to lunch.

I wasn't hungry at all but chewed quickly, tearing into my sandwich, as if making it disappear would make the eerie feeling in the air disappear with it.

Vic nearly landed in my lap when she scrambled over to our table, late, bursting at the seams to discuss the news.

"Can you believe it?"

"Believe what?" I asked, my face as blank as the paper bag I'd thrown my lunch in that morning.

"How did you *not* hear?" Vic wanted to know. "I do everything humanly possible to avoid all drama at this school and even *I* heard."

I shook my head to show I still didn't know what she was talking about.

"Trina"—she ripped open the Velcro seal on her lunch bag for effect—"is in the principal's office."

My face froze. My jaw muscles forgot what they were doing, and I nearly choked on the wad of bread in my mouth.

"And her parents just got here, too. My entire gym class saw them waiting in the office when we were coming back inside. She must be in *big* trouble," Vic explained. "You know all the cheating on the midterms they never could pin on anyone?" she prodded.

My eyes dried up in an instant. I couldn't blink and I

couldn't swallow and my ears suddenly felt clogged, so every word Vic said next sounded elongated.

"Everyone's saying it must have been Trina. Why else would her parents be here?" Vic's dark hair was frizzing out of her ponytail in every direction, the way it always did by this time of day.

"Trey's in the office, too," she added, "but we know he didn't do it. No way would Trey cheat." Vic made her *duh* face. "You would never fall for *that* kind of guy."

The small bits of sandwich left in my mouth turned to sand and lodged in my throat like a warning.

And then the vice principal walked into the lunchroom, scanned the space, and zeroed in on me.

"Jamie Bunn, we need you in the office. Right now."

Vic's eyes nearly popped out of her head, and her mouth fell open so wide I could see the fillings in her molars. Every set of eyes in the cafeteria was fixed on me.

I stood up slowly, my limbs moving as if underwater.

Vic put her hand on my wrist. "Jamie?" she questioned, my name sounding foreign, even to me.

I shook my head and opened my mouth, but nothing came out. Then I tried again and managed to get out one sad, simple word: "Sorry."

The bells on the library door jingled and broke my train of

thought. I looked at the clock to orient myself. It was 4:22 now, and still no Black Hat Guy. I looked at the chair again. The sun would keep moving across the sky, the ray of light would keep shifting. It would soon fall across a different collection of words that might or might not be another comment on my life.

I was starting to really hate that chair.

I took the opportunity to dust the shelves behind the empty chair, the windowsill next to it, and the baseboard molding. Then I brushed off the thin line of dust that had collected on the top edge of the new outlet where Black Hat Guy plugged in his phone. What would he do if he didn't recharge his phone today? He was so dependent on it, as if it kept him alive as much as food and water and oxygen did. I felt a small panic for him and hoped he was somewhere with an outlet.

"Jamie," Sonia called. "Feel like checking the book drops?"

"Sure," I answered. I handed my cleaning supplies over the counter, and Sonia handed a bag to me.

"If it's really full, make more than one trip, mami. Don't kill yourself lugging them all at once."

"I won't. Thanks."

I listened to the familiar jingle of the bells as I opened the door and stepped into the muggy afternoon air. It felt like rain was on its way. Most people complained about rain, but I loved it. I loved the smell of rain, before and during, but mostly after, how nothing else in the world smelled just like it. I loved how the shade of every color changed in the rain to a softer version of itself. But most of all, I loved the way the world got quiet for rain. Like library quiet.

I ambled around the building to the book drops.

And there was Shady.

He was tucked between the two drops, same as before, but this time up on all fours and busy at work. He was licking a clear plastic plate that looked like the lid of a takeout container. Shady looked very satisfied with whatever it was he had just devoured. He pattered over on his small dirty paws to wag his tail at me, sniff my sandaled feet, and lick my hand once I bent down to him. I saw the makeshift water cup had been replaced with a round black shallow bowl—the bottom of the takeout container. It was full of clean water, filled to the brim, with three ice cubes floating on the surface like tiny logs in a lake. Someone had just visited this little guy.

Shady turned then and padded his way back to his spot, spiraled in a circle twice, then plopped down and closed his eyes.

"All right, cutie. Nap time for you." I emptied the drops and carried the returns back inside.

I stacked the books on the counter for Sonia and felt myself do an actual double take as I spotted Black Hat Guy in his chair. He was seated, one leg crossed over the other, his phone plugged into the newly cleaned outlet, typing and scrolling on the tiny screen.

"Did he just get here?" I whispered to Sonia.

"Yes. Late today," she said.

"I was worried about him," I admitted.

"Just late." Sonia was busy typing up the calendar part of the library newsletter. "Maybe tonight's a full moon."

"A full moon?" I repeated.

"Hmmm." She kept working, eyes on the screen.

"What, like he's a werewolf?"

"Huh? What are you talking about?" Sonia stopped typing and looked at me like I was nuts.

"Nothing, sorry."

After Sonia checked in the books from the drop, I lined them up on the shelving cart. I was about to arrange them in order by call number, but my eye jumped to a title instead, and then the next title, and then the one after that.

"Oh my gosh," I said. "Sonia, look at this!" I pointed at the last three books and said, "If you read these titles in order, it says '*Between You and Me, Who Will Run the Frog Hospital?, Just Kids.*' Isn't that funny? It's like a little story."

"It's spine poetry," Sonia answered back. "It's a thing."

"What's a thing?"

"Exactly what you just did, arranging a stack of books so

the titles on the spine read from top to bottom like a poem."

"But I didn't do this. They were already in that order."

"Hmmm." Sonia thought, moving her eyebrows up and down in challenge. "Sounds like it's time for a new game."

Sonia was awesome.

"Okay," I agreed.

"One hour. That's it. Then we'll show each other what we've got. You can use the purple cart in the back room to store your poems, and I'll stick mine under the counter. Starting"— she squinted at the clock above the door—"now!"

I rushed to the back room to grab the cart and tackle some shelf reading while I played the game. Maybe I'd get lucky and find books next to each other that already worked as a poem. But then I thought that sounded a little like cheating, and I would never do anything even remotely close to cheating again, so I bagged that idea and just looked for interesting titles.

After only a few minutes, though, Beverly found me and gave me a long list of picture books and novels to pull out of the kids' collection. Sonia got pretty busy at the circ desk, too, and I noticed her step toward the stacks only a handful of times to grab books, which made me feel better, because spine poetry was a lot harder than I thought it'd be.

I wasn't much of a poetry reader, so I didn't have the first idea how to write a poem. Plus, I kept getting interrupted—I had to empty the book drops again, and I had to double-check a stack of easy readers. I also had to put together seven different puzzles some kid pulled apart and left scattered all over the floor.

"Time's up!" Sonia announced, sticking her head into the children's room. "We went over, actually."

"That went too fast," I said.

"Because it was fun. Meet me out front with your poems," and she returned to the circ desk.

I didn't need a cart to carry my spine poems. I had only managed to make one.

"Okay, show me what you got," Sonia said when I reached her. She was sitting on the tall stool, swinging her feet like an overexcited kid.

"Um, can you go first?"

"Certainly," she said, sounding a little too eager to show me her work. She thumped her first stack onto the counter for me to read, lining them up just so. There were only three titles in her first poem. I read them out loud:

Wild Swans
The Color of Water
Dance Dance Dance

"That's really beautiful." I was in awe.

"I know."

"That really sounds like a poem," I said.

"I know."

"Gee, Sonia. Modest at all?"

"Not with this. I rock at spine poetry," she said confidently. "Own up when you're good at something. It's not bragging. It's just honesty."

"Okay . . ." I considered that.

"Like with your artwork, what I saw in your sketchbook. You're good. You don't have to be shy about it."

"Really?"

"That's exactly what I'm talking about. *Yes, really.* Own it."

"Okay," I said, more sure this time. "Thank you."

"Ready for my next one? I made three total."

Sonia set up a stack of five books, then read it to me:

Breath, Eyes, Memory
Hold Still
Wise Children
Quiet
Kiss Good Night

"You're so good at this!" I almost yelled at her.

She just started laughing, while she reached for another stack. "Last one."

One Crazy Summer
A Walk in the Woods
Why We Broke Up
Forever
Farewell, My Lovely

"Okay, you killed me in this game. I'm dead. So dead."

Sonia was still laughing. "Show me yours. I bet it's great."

I let out a heavy breath and bit my lip. I couldn't believe what I was about to reveal, especially after Sonia's gorgeous work.

"Fine. Here it is." And I set it up on the counter next to hers, just one book on top of another:

The Trouble with Chickens
Scat

And Sonia erupted, laughter shooting out of her in every possible direction. She doubled over, clutching her stomach, and I couldn't help it, I burst into laughter, too.

Within a minute Lenny was there, checking to see what all the noise was about. One glance at the stacks of books as he approached us and he said, "Spine poetry? I love spine poetry."

Sonia just pointed at my puny stack, unable to get out

actual words because of the laughing.

Lenny read it and let out a howl, cracking up as hard as Sonia.

"Chickens," he managed to say between laughs, "and fecal matter." He tried to whisper, but the heavy breathing that went with the laughter made it hard to keep quiet. "That's poetry gold."

I smiled wide at my two new friends and shrugged. I guess I knew how to write a poem after all.

Sonia

→→→·←←←

After a rush of patrons right at opening the next morning, the library emptied out and I had time to browse the Art section. It was Wednesday, July 26, which also happened to be National Aunt and Uncle Day. I wanted to make a special drawing for my aunt Julie, so was searching for some inspiration. I couldn't believe I had lived in Foxfield all these years and never knew about the gorgeous art books sitting on these shelves, waiting for me the whole time. I had a lot of catching up to do. Before I picked one to take home, though, Sonia called me over to the circ desk.

"We're slow right now. You want to do this pile of returns yourself?" she asked me, sipping coffee in a mug that read *I'd rather be in the library.*

"Really?" I asked, excited to learn something new.

"I'll watch you. It'll be fine." Sonia half glared at me, and then ordered, "Have some confidence."

"Okay."

"Trade spots." Sonia switched places with me so I was behind the monitor. "Hit F2 to get to the check-in screen, then click here to set it up for this pile."

I followed her directions.

"Now it's just the same as you did last time. Scan each one, make sure you get a beep, and read the title on the screen."

"Okay, I can do that." I picked up the first book.

"Of course you can." Sonia pulled up a chair and sat beside me, ready to watch over my shoulder as I worked. "Then when you finish this pile, we'll scan them again under inventory check, to make sure they're all in. Always double-check."

"Always double-check," I repeated. "That's what your mug should say, by the way."

"What?"

"Your mug. What it says doesn't make any sense, that you'd 'rather be in the library,' because you *are* in the library. It's confusing. You should have one that says 'Always double-check.' That would be better."

"I think you're taking my mug situation too seriously," Sonia replied.

I smiled to myself, then got to work.

I scanned and it beeped and I read the screen, and then I placed the book in a pile to my right. I got a rhythm down—scan, beep, read, place, scan, beep, read, place—and it was downright fun. I stood taller and pushed my shoulders back.

Scan, beep, read, place.

I looked up from the screen when a mom came in with a young boy, grubby with kid sweat and dirt on his little knees. I greeted them and they said hello back and then walked over to the children's room. An older couple, Mr. and Mrs. Jansen, came in right after them. They chose some back issues of *Reader's Digest* from the periodical wall and settled into seats side by side to read them.

I kept going with my pile, slowing down a bit on purpose to make it last. These patrons who walked in and saw me behind the desk thought I was a regular library employee. Why wouldn't they? I was doing the work and I was dressing the part and I really felt, for the first time in a long time, like I was part of something good. I didn't want it to end.

Scan, beep, read—

And then it ended.

The title on the screen: *Jane Eyre.*

My gut clenched and twisted as I stared at it.

"It went through," Sonia said. "What's wrong?"

I held up the book so the cover faced her.

"Oh," she said.

Sonia put her coffee cup aside and leaned closer to me. "Okay. Should we talk this out, Jamie?"

"No," I mumbled.

"No?"

"It's fine. I'm fine," I lied.

"You're lying," she said.

"Beverly already talked to me," I said.

"Well, it appears there are some loose ends still tangling you up. Otherwise, I'd still be hearing that beautiful sound of books beeping back into the collection." Sonia stared at me.

"You don't have to," I answered, not looking at her.

"Of course I don't, and you don't have to be doing my job right now, but you are. You're already past your hours this week, *again*. We both know that."

"I like it here," I said quietly, staring at my sandals and the worn, scratched tile beneath them.

"And we like *you*, but you can't spend the rest of your life afraid of a book title." Sonia hopped off her chair to grab an empty stool on wheels and rolled it over to me.

"Sit," she commanded. Then she positioned her chair so we were facing each other, our knees touching, our faces less than two feet apart.

"So let's start with the girl who asked for this book—every

time she comes in here, you freeze up like a mouse dropped in a snake cage."

I tilted my head and squinted my eyes, trying to figure out exactly what that meant.

"Don't ask," Sonia warned.

I furrowed my eyebrows, asking.

"My son, Mateo, went through a snake phase, a *pet* snake phase." She shook her head as if casting away a bad memory. "It didn't last long. One feeding and it was over."

I grimaced.

"So, that girl?"

"That's Trina," I said. "She's in my grade. She's Trey's sister."

"Who's Trey?" Sonia asked.

I sighed heavily. "It's too embarrassing."

"It *was* embarrassing," Sonia corrected me. "Now it's over. It's been over for a long time, but you won't let it go. It's like you have this whole fantastic book in front of you, but you just keep reading the same awful chapter over and over again. It's time to turn the page, mami, and get on with the next part of the story." Sonia let out a deep breath.

"Besides, a mistake over a boy is a rite of passage." She nodded with certainty. "Trust me. I know."

"I still feel stupid," I mumbled.

"Yeah? Go see how far that gets you. You think I felt like

a world scholar when Mateo's father disappeared one day, taking all my money with him, me only nineteen years old with a growing bowling ball in my belly and all alone?" She kept her voice low so only I could hear. "It happened. You keep going. You turn the page."

"Well now I *really* feel stupid, compared to what you had to go through. . . ."

"Don't feel stupid. Just get it out of your system once and for all and be done with it."

The mom with the little boy returned to the desk with two movies to check out.

Sonia stepped in front of the monitor to help them.

"Just these today. I have a project to get through tonight and I need him out of my hair," the mom explained to us, guilt in her voice.

"Mommy, I want books," the boy whined.

"Next time, Xander. I promise. We're in a rush now."

Xander whined more.

"My kid wants a book and I'm making him get movies," she said, digging her library card out of her wallet. "I guess I'll be receiving the Mom of the Year Award."

"No, no," Sonia told her. "You do what you have to do." She scanned the woman's card and movies and handed them back to her.

"Mo-om," Xander groaned.

Sonia leaned over the counter to tell the little boy, "The next time you come I will have a stack of *new* books, just for you, okay?"

He stared back up at her, eyes wide, lips parted.

"Oh, Xander, isn't that special? New books just for you!" his mom repeated.

"Okay, Xander?" Sonia said, smiling her gorgeous smile at him.

"O-kay," he answered back.

"Thank you so much," the mom gushed at Sonia.

"Of course. You're welcome."

"Let's go, sweet pea." The mom corralled him toward the door.

"Thank you," she called again over the door jingle.

"Bye, Xander," Sonia called, waving as he stepped backward out the door.

"You're so good with everyone," I told Sonia, once the door closed behind them.

"It's a gift," she said, then asked, as if there had been no interruption, "So how is Trina involved?"

"Trina busted me. Trina's the reason I'm here all summer."

"Then I love Trina! Trina is my favorite!" Sonia chirped.

I couldn't help smiling, but I shook my head at the same time.

"Spill it," Sonia ordered.

"Okay, the short version is this. I took the copy of *Jane Eyre* from the library, which was stealing. I snuck it into Trey's backpack because all the exam answers were in it, which was cheating. Trina turned it in and told on me, which was"—I held up my hands to make air quotes—"'excelling in school citizenship.'" I dropped my hands. "So she's the hero, Trey's the innocent victim, and I'm the criminal."

That was it, in a nutshell. But there was no nutshell big enough to contain how stupid and horrible I felt about it.

"So, not your finest decision-making," Sonia stated.

"Nope," I agreed. "Especially since we have this big-deal zero tolerance Honor Code at school and there was already a cheating scandal this year, on the midterms. But no one got busted. The principal and teachers were going crazy trying to piece it together and figure out who was responsible, but they never could."

"They were outsmarted by the cheaters," Sonia summarized.

"Exactly. It was like some bad teen movie where the administration becomes the laughingstock of the school and the sneaky kids get away scot-free."

"I remember reading something about that in the *Biweekly*," Sonia admitted.

"They were trying to get the guilty parties to confess for a more lenient punishment," I explained. "That's how desperate they were."

Sonia raised her eyebrows at me, and I shook my head in response. "It didn't work. No one came forward."

"Okay," Sonia said, clapping her hands together once, "thank you for providing context, but I would like to get back to discussing you."

"I wouldn't," I replied.

Sonia ignored me and instead pronounced, "So, since the book at the center of all this drama is *Jane Eyre*, we will break it all down in *Jane Eyre* terms."

"What?" I had no idea what she was talking about.

"Relax. This is very straightforward."

"You've read *Jane Eyre*?" I asked, still confused.

"Jamie, they were teaching Jane Eyre in eighth grade back when *I* was a kid in the middle school. I grew up here, remember?"

"Oh yeah." I made a *duh* face, which reminded me of Vic. Vic would really like Sonia, I realized.

"I've also spent the bulk of my life in a library. I've read pretty much everything."

"Bragger," I teased.

"Now try to follow me," Sonia ordered, and then she zoomed ahead. "The school sees it that Trina is Jane, the honest, dignified heroine who does the right thing, Trey is Mr. Rochester, the innocent victim who had no idea what was coming his way, and you are Bertha, the nightmare in the attic who causes all the trouble."

"I'm Bertha?" I asked, my voice flat. "Didn't you say you wanted to help me feel better about all this?"

"Of course."

"I can't feel better if I'm Bertha."

"You can't feel better because you already see yourself as Bertha—you didn't need me to say it."

I sat with that for a minute. She was probably right. I had been punishing myself all summer long, hiding at home when I wasn't working at the library, living like a nocturnal animal. I hadn't had a sleepover at Aunt Julie's house once since school ended, and I wasn't even writing Vic letters the way I promised I would.

It was getting old. In fact, it was way past old.

I cleared my throat. "Well, I don't want to be Bertha anymore," I said, and I really meant it.

"Glad to hear it, because Bertha has serious medical issues and was the victim of other people's cruel choices and can't help herself, but you can. You are not Bertha. If you are anyone in that book, you are Jane."

"Oh no," I protested. "I don't think I'm Jane."

"You could be Jane," Sonia assured me. "Trina doesn't get to be Jane. In fact, she doesn't get to be in your story at all."

"Oh, she's in it," I muttered. My eyes started to well immediately, just at the memory.

"Oh no, mami. That bad?"

I nodded yes and told her about Trina posting my apology letter to Trey on a public Instagram account opened just for middle school drama. It was quickly shut down, of course, but not in time to stop a gazillion people from taking screenshots of the letter and sharing it over and over.

Sonia said something in Spanish then that she refused to translate for me.

"And that wasn't even enough for her." I swallowed down the lump forming in the back of my throat. "A week after the whole thing, I went to my locker to pack up and when I opened it all these trays, these plastic trays from the lunchroom, came crashing out at me."

Sonia's eyes pinched and little lines formed above her perfect eyebrows.

"And then soda cans came rolling out also, cans of Crush soda, and some of them split when they hit the floor and the orange soda went spurting everywhere and I was soaked and everyone in the hallway was dying laughing at me."

"Trays for Trey, and orange Crush soda for your crush on

him." Sonia processed it out loud slowly. "You gotta give her credit for creativity." She shook her head in disbelief.

"And then there were the bathroom stalls."

"Go on," Sonia urged.

"Vic told me there was graffiti about me in two stalls in the bathroom on the third floor. She tried to erase it, but it was in permanent marker and she couldn't get it off."

After Vic told me, it took me two days to build up the nerve to look, but once I did, I found it easily in the first stall, in neatly written black Sharpie: *Worried about exams? Need a ~~tutor~~ cheater? Call Jamie Bunn.*

The second stall said, in brown marker: *Feel CONNECTED to someone who DOESN'T like you back? Join the Jamie Bunn club!*

I could still see my name on the wall, glaring at me.

"Okay, this Trina is a real piece of work." Sonia reached over and hugged me tight to her. I breathed in her sweet smell, a mix of books and coffee and lip gloss.

"But she won't always be like that, you know," Sonia said, very matter-of-factly. "It won't last."

"Like the pet snake thing?" I asked.

"Exactly."

"You don't know Trina. It might last."

"Maybe you don't know Trina, either."

I looked at the floor and admitted to myself that it was

true—I didn't really know Trina. But it was because she was too mean to get to know. She scared me.

"So let's just focus on Trey now," Sonia advised. "He's the Mr. Rochester in your story."

I considered it, but then had to admit, "I don't think Trey is like Mr. Rochester."

"Is Trey moody? Or hot-tempered? Or hiding his wife in his attic?"

"No, no, and definitely no."

"Is Trey someone you can't get out of your mind, no matter how hard you try?"

I paused.

Then I told the truth. "Yes."

"Then he is Mr. Rochester. Don't argue." Sonia sat up straight and tall, looking very pleased with her analysis, and sipped more of her coffee.

"So that means I'm going to end up with Trey and live happily ever after with him, just like Jane does with Mr. Rochester."

"No." Sonia shot me down without a blink, disapproval in her voice. "It means you will live happily ever after with *yourself*, which is all that matters. Learn from your mistakes and live the life you believe in. The boy in the story is just a side note."

"The boy in the *Jane Eyre* story or the boy in my story?" I asked, getting confused.

"Both. Neither. It doesn't matter." She waved her hands in front of her as if smacking away gnats. "The story is about *you*. *You* made a mistake. *You* served your time. Now move on. Turn the page."

I took a deep breath and let this sink in.

Sonia waited, watching me.

"Anyway, that's what I did, and look at me now." She hopped off her chair and shook off her serious vibe like a dog shaking water off its fur. Then she struck a pose like one of those gorgeous marble statues from the sculpture books in the 730s.

I looked at Sonia's pose, how confident she seemed, and thought about what she was saying. I realized that my mom had done exactly what Sonia was telling me to do. She recognized the mistake she made with my dad, so she folded her hand and then she fixed it. She started over and built herself the life she wanted. I guessed my dad was her *rite of passage* mistake. And when my mom curled up in my bed with me, two weeks after her meeting with Mrs. Shupe, and told me, "You played cards you didn't have and you lost. I know it hurts, but that's how you learn. In fact, that might be the *very best* way to learn," I knew she forgave me the same way she had forgiven herself, years ago, for my dad.

My mom had turned the page.

So had Sonia.

I could, too.

"Sonia?" I said quietly.

She dropped her pose and looked at me, warmth radiating off her. "Yes, Jamie?" She took my hand in hers. I felt a surge of strength rush from her skin to mine.

I squeezed her hand gently. "Thanks for being my compass."

"You're very welcome, mami." Sonia gave my hand a slow, tender squeeze back and then let go.

Beverly

>>>·<<<

L ater that afternoon, I knocked on Beverly's office door with my free hand.

"Yes? Come in."

She was sitting at her desk, a pencil in her hand and another tucked behind her ear. She was working through a huge stack of papers. She hadn't emerged in almost two hours, which was unheard-of for Beverly. I was used to her making constant rounds, checking on everything and everyone throughout the building.

"Sorry to interrupt, but Lenny wanted me to bring you this." I was delivering another homemade treat. This time they were muffins, three on a biodegradable paper plate. The nest cookies had been a huge hit—Sonia loved them—which inspired Lenny to experiment even more. These muffins were made with zucchini and carrot and beet and sweet potato, which sounded suspicious, but somehow worked really well. The brown-sugar crumb topping he decided to add last minute was a smart choice. I told him that.

"Oh, how lovely," Beverly said. She took the plate from me and said, "Why don't you take a seat and have one with me? I could use the break."

"Sure," I agreed, and sat in the chair on the other side of her desk.

Beverly pulled a tissue from the box on her desk and placed a muffin on it, then slid the plate toward me so I could choose my own. She examined her muffin, squinting as she studied it, inspecting it like it was a rare specimen retrieved from another planet. Still peering at the muffin before her, she asked, "Have you had one yet?"

The way she said it, and the way she was staring it down, I couldn't help it—I laughed.

Loud.

Beverly looked at me in surprise, then broke into a big smile herself. "Well," she said. Her shoulders dropped, and the wrinkles around her eyes smoothed out a bit as she relaxed. "You can't blame me for asking."

"Actually," I told her, "they're really good."

"Really?"

"I say they're tied with last week's lumpy chocolate oatmeal cookies, and those were great, remember?" All of a sudden, it felt like I was talking to Vic at the lunch table, not my fifty-something-year-old boss at the library.

Beverly started to peel the wrapper off her muffin. "Lenny really has taught himself to be quite the baker. I don't know where he finds the time."

I started in on my muffin, even though I had just eaten one downstairs with Lenny before coming to Beverly's office. Who would have ever thought I would meet my daily vegetable requirements by eating muffins?

"That looks fun," I said, gesturing to the stack of papers full of dense black print on Beverly's desk.

"Oh, yes, well." Beverly glanced at the stack with a sad look on her face. "Policy and regulations and financing."

"Sorry, that sounds awful," I admitted.

"It kind of is. But I need to review it all. I have a meeting later today with library directors from two other towns who also had to fight to keep their libraries open. And they won, so hopefully they'll be able to help us." She stopped then to gather her thoughts, her gaze locked on her muffin. She pinched a piece of crumb topping between two fingers.

"People here are already mad about us being closed on weekends—I've heard them complain," I said. "Imagine how mad they'll be if we close completely?"

"Yes, as they should be. It was bad enough when they limited our hours. But this new mayor, Trippley, he never said anything about cutting the library when he was campaigning for office. And now, all of a sudden, it's one of his main goals."

"Sonia doesn't like him," I said.

Beverly smiled at that. "Well, Sonia loves her library, and I do, too, and it's my job to take care of it. I've been through this before, you know, when I lived in Ohio. I was the director there for six years before the library closed. It was devastating. We all lost our jobs and the town lost its community center. I don't want to see that happen again." She gazed out the window for a short moment, then came back, waved a hand at the stack of papers on her desk, and said, "So, I'm not going to let it happen again."

The fight in Beverly's voice gave me hope.

She smiled at me and took a bite of her muffin. I was already half-finished with mine.

"Lenny suggested setting up a small café corner in the library, where he could sell his baked goods and we could set up a coffee station, to raise money," Beverly said.

"That sounds great."

"Well, possibly." She tapped the stack of papers. "Everything has its rules and regulations, so that's another project to research. But I'm working on it. For Lenny."

"So there's a lot more to running a library than people know," I admitted. "It's not just about the books and movies and magazines."

"No. I wish it were," Beverly said.

"Because that's the fun part. The books and the movies. And the organizing. I had so much fun when Sonia let me check in books the other day. It reminded me of playing house with my friend Vic when we were little."

Beverly smiled and listened to me ramble on while she chewed.

"We would play house and we were the adults, so we called all the shots, and that feeling, you know, of being grown up and in charge was so great, like we were so important and special. And when I started checking in the books at the circ desk, I felt that exact same way again, at least for a few minutes."

I could see my reflection in the glassy lenses of Beverly's eyes and wondered if she could see herself in mine.

She brushed her crumbs into a small pile with her fingertips, slowly, like brushing sand off a fossil. Her hands were small and delicate, the skin so milky pale they almost had a glow to them.

Then she said, "I know exactly what you mean. I used to play library with my little sister. She would push our tea table up to her bedroom door and set her books in perfect rows on it. She'd ring a bell to announce that the library was open. She was always the librarian and I was always the patron. I had to browse the books, even though I knew them all inside and out. Then I would hand her three to check out—she only allowed me three at a time. That was a very strict rule." Beverly paused here to sigh and smile a half smile. "She loved her rules."

I smiled, and Beverly continued, "She put index cards in the back of each book and had a rubber stamp, but no ink—my mom was fussy and wouldn't allow ink—and she would fake-stamp each book and then make me sign a 'promise to return' sheet. She was very organized, very systematic about the procedure. She loved the precision, the order, the share-and-return aspect of it. It was her favorite game in the whole world. Even back then, she said she was going to be a librarian when she grew up. And she meant it." Beverly leaned forward on her desk toward me and nodded. "I'm sure playing library brought her that same feeling, of being grown up and important and in charge. That's an important feeling when you're little."

"I never thought of playing library," I admitted. "Just house and supermarket. Oh, and shoe store! Shoe store was really fun. But I never did library." I was making up for it by working in a real library now, though, which had to be just as good. Or even better.

Beverly nodded at me and said, in a distant voice, "My sister would *only* play library."

"And now you're a librarian for real. See how that worked out?" I loved how much sense that made. "Is your sister a librarian now, too?" I asked.

And just like that, the color drained from Beverly's face and her torso stiffened.

"Is something—" I started to ask, but a loud knock on the door interrupted me.

Lenny poked his head in. "I just wanted to see what you thought of my— Oh God." He stopped once he saw the look on Beverly's face. "They're not that bad, are they?"

Beverly startled, looked perplexed for a quick second, then recovered.

"No, no," she said.

"Are you okay?" Lenny asked.

"Yes. And the muffins—they're delicious, Lenny," she said, nodding first at the crumb-covered tissue before her and then at him. "Very delicious."

Lenny relaxed into his regular easygoing self again. "Thank you. So, you think people would pay for them?" he asked, excitement blooming in his voice.

"I would," Beverly answered, smiling and nodding more. Her shoulders softened.

"I would, too," I answered.

"Great! There are more down in the kitchen, so please help yourself." And he disappeared out of the doorway.

I looked at Beverly, hoping to finish our conversation, but before I could say a word, Lenny popped his head back in.

"On second thought," he said, "you might want to go easy on them. They kind of wreak havoc on your gut if you eat too many at a time." Lenny put a hand across his stomach to illustrate his point. "There's a lot of fiber in those babies." He gave us a thumbs-up sign, and then said, "All right. Thanks." And he popped out again.

Beverly and I looked at each other.

"I only had one," Beverly volunteered, relief flooding her face.

"I had two. I'm done," I stated, pushing the plate with the remaining muffin away from my side of the desk.

"I'm sure you'll be fine," Beverly reassured me.

"Two isn't too much?" I asked nervously.

"Two is perfect," she said, reaching for her locket and sliding it along its chain before dropping it back beneath her shirt. Then she clapped her hands together and announced, "Snack time's over! Back to work now for both of us."

I cleaned up my crumbs and headed back to the circ desk. And so far my stomach felt fine.

Black Hat Guy

>>>·<<<

The next day at 4:05 Black Hat Guy swung into the library, sort of bouncing in a way I'd never seen him do before. He quickly claimed his quotes chair, leaning his backpack against the leg and plugging his phone cord into the usual outlet under the window. He left the phone on the seat of the chair, resting like a cat in the sun, and walked over to the circulation desk. I watched from my spot by the magazines, where I was putting issues in chronological order.

"Hey, how you doing, man?" Lenny greeted him, reaching over the counter to shake Black Hat Guy's hand. Sonia was downstairs, refilling her coffee.

"All right, man, all right," Black Hat Guy answered, his neck straightening up out of his sweatshirt collar like a turtle stretching out of its shell.

"What can I do for you?" Lenny had gray-and-brown stubble growing on the bottom half of his face, and he rubbed his palm against it while he waited for Black Hat Guy to respond.

"I was wondering if you had some books." He reached into his pocket and pulled out a crumpled piece of paper. He flattened it out on the counter and then handed it to Lenny, asking, "Do you have either of these?"

"Let's see." Lenny typed something into his computer. "We have that first one, but not the second. That first one is in. Come with me, I'll show you where."

"Thanks, man."

"No problem. That's what we do." He gave Black Hat Guy a pat on the shoulder. "Jamie, keep an eye on the desk for me?"

"Sure," I called back.

As Lenny walked him back to the stacks, I heard him ask, "You getting a pet or something?"

"No, nothing like that. Just curious about some stuff." Black Hat Guy's voice trailed off as he followed Lenny to the back room.

I was working on a mess of *New Yorker* magazines that had piled up on the magazine rack when Sonia returned to the circ desk, coffee cup in hand.

"Those brownies downstairs, Jamie, did you try them?" Sonia asked from the desk. "Or whatever they are, I don't know. They're excellent, though."

"Yes," I answered. "I've had two."

She made a face. "That Lenny's gonna make me fat."

"I doubt that," I laughed.

"Every day he brings a new treat!"

"Maybe we can ask him to bring carrot sticks once in a while then," I suggested.

"And then he'll bake them in coconut sugar and hand-tapped maple syrup!"

I laughed because she was right. He probably would.

I heaved the newly organized pile of magazines back into its shelf space and arched my back to stretch. Who knew working at the library would make my muscles sore?

"I'm gonna check the book drops, Sonia."

"Let me go. I need to walk off my brownie thingie." She grabbed the bag and hurried from behind the desk. "I hope it's loaded so I have to make two trips. Or three trips. Or maybe I'll just walk around the building a few times. That might be good."

"Oh my God, Sonia."

"I'm going. See you in a few."

"Fine." I waved. "Bye."

Black Hat Guy emerged from the back room, a book in hand, and headed back to his chair. When he sat, his leg blocked the ending of a quote running across the bottom of the seat, leaving it to say only *If you look for perfection, you'll never be.* Black Hat Guy turned a page and kept reading.

"How's your day been, Jamie?" Lenny asked as he returned to the desk.

"So far so good," I answered. "Is he going to check that out?" I pointed my chin at Black Hat Guy.

"Nah, just using it here," Lenny answered. "He can't borrow it."

"Why not?"

Lenny turned his back to Black Hat Guy and lowered his voice. "He doesn't have a library card."

"But he's here all the time. Why wouldn't he have a card?"

"You need to have a residence in town to have a card."

"Oh. So he doesn't live here," I concluded.

"Actually, he doesn't really live anywhere," Lenny said. "Nowhere permanent."

"Like, he's homeless?"

"At the moment, yes. But he's staying at his buddy's place right now—or in his garage."

"Garage?" I mouthed.

"Rick's wife is not on board and has no idea. If she finds out, he'll need a new plan. But right now, Rick leaves the garage unlocked so he can slip in at night and then slip out in the morning."

"He doesn't have any family to go to?"

"He's burned some bridges, from what I gather, so no, he's on his own. He's lucky he has that friend, though, and his garage."

What would happen the day Rick's wife had some special appointment and needed her car super early in the morning? Black Hat Guy would get busted and lose his only shelter for good? What then? He would have nowhere to go. Except the library. He could spend his days in the library, of course, but not the nights. Where would he go at night?

I really hoped Rick's wife liked to sleep in.

"I know he looks peculiar, sitting in that same spot, using that same outlet every single day, but I think going to that chair makes him feel like he has a place of his own. And the phone, well, that's all he's got."

I peeked around Lenny's shoulder to look at Black Hat Guy again. He was busy at work, focused on his book, his finger moving along the page in sync with his eyes.

"That phone"—Lenny kept talking—"that's his news, his emails, all his contacts, his internet, television."

"I get it. It makes sense," I said quietly. "Thanks for telling me, Lenny. I had no idea."

"There's no way you could have known. I just found out myself." He shrugged.

"So how can we help him?"

"We've been helping him. He needs the library, and we keep it here for him. We welcome him. We didn't need to know his story to help him." Lenny paused, then added, "We just need to remember that everyone has one."

Black Hat Guy, Wally, Sonia, Lenny, Beverly, Jane Eyre, who still counted even though she was a fictional character.

Me.

Everyone had a story.

"And you found out all this how?" I asked.

"I found out because he started telling me. I bumped into him at the Bean Pot." Lenny pursed his lips together, then said, "Sometimes you just need to talk, and I happened to be there, so . . ."

"No way, Lenny. It didn't *just happen* to be you. He talked *because* it was you. Sonia says you are the bartender of libraries."

Lenny took a step back.

"Sonia said that?" he asked.

"She always says that. She says you're the easiest person to talk to in the world and that you have this way of making everyone feel comfortable and that you're pretty much the best listener ever."

Lenny's eyes opened wide. "Wow, I never knew she thought that."

"Well, she does!"

"See what we have here?" Lenny bounced on his feet a little.

"What?"

"An exchange of information." Lenny was getting punchy. "Sharing is caring. You share with me, I share with you. We all pay it forward. The skies rain compassion. It's a win-win-win-win-win."

I laughed, then quickly lowered my voice when a patron on a computer looked up at me in irritation. I mouthed "Sorry" at him and then whisper-laughed to Lenny, "What are you even talking about?"

"I am talking about the rush of joy I am feeling at this momentous moment," Lenny answered me. "I must bake. I am feeling a spectacular need to bake!" His eyes jumped to the clock above the library door entrance. "And how about that for the world being in sync—look at the time!"

"You're done for the day?"

"I am done for the day." He paused, then cackled a fake witch laugh and rubbed his hands together devilishly. "Or am I?"

I rolled my eyes. "Okay, Lenny. Go home and bake something delicious."

"I shall," he replied.

"With chocolate."

"As you wish," he said, bowing at the waist.

Lenny quickly logged his hours into the time sheet, gathered up his things from under the circ desk, and rounded his way from behind the counter.

"Oh, but what about his book?" I asked quietly, nodding toward Black Hat Guy. "You said I can't check it out to him."

"He won't ask you to. Just shelve it and we'll pull it for him again tomorrow if he wants."

"Got it. Have a good night." I smiled at him.

"You, too. Have a *great* one." Lenny waved at me enthusiastically.

Black Hat Guy looked up as Lenny opened the library door. He lifted his hand and called, "Bye, man. Thanks."

Lenny gave a big wave and replied with, "Anytime. See you later."

Black Hat Guy's eyes quickly darted over to mine after the door closed, and he caught me staring at him. I smiled, my lips pressed together in an effort to look professional and welcoming, like Sonia. I was trying to look like I *hadn't* just learned some seriously private and personal information about him. After all, I knew firsthand what it felt like to have seriously private and personal information shared with the public. I wasn't about to make him feel the way I had at school.

Black Hay Guy's mouth twitched into a half smile in return. Then he lowered his head and got back to work.

My eyes wandered around the room and settled on a small empty space near Black Hat Guy's chair. There was just enough room there for a table with a platter of baked goods, a coffeepot, and some cups and napkins, like Lenny had suggested to Beverly. I hoped we would be able to set it up.

The community bulletin board looked like it hadn't been cleaned off in a while. It hung on the wall by the entrance, and I could see from my spot at the desk that it was drowning under layers of notices. The flyers were ripped, wrinkled, and curling up on themselves. From this angle, the board looked a lot like a giant paper sculpture one of the eighth graders made in Art Club last year.

I began leafing through the piles of papers thumbtacked crookedly on top of each other. Only director-approved notices were allowed up on the board, mostly just ads for town events and nonprofit groups, but tons of people came with thumbtacks and stuck up their own personal notices anyway. It was my job to weed those out, and also pull down flyers for events that had long passed, like the Earth Day event back in April and the Memorial Day Parade ad from May.

It took a good ten minutes to go through the whole board, remove the junk and dated material, and then rehang the current news neatly. I took my stack of old papers to the recycling bin and saw that Black Hat Guy's chair was empty. He was probably in the bathroom. The book was closed, his phone shoved like a bookmark inside to hold his page. I recognized the cover immediately because my aunt Julie had a copy of the same book at her house. The title was *Everything You Need to Know About Dogs*.

AUGUST

Wally

-›››·‹‹‹-

I t was the first day of August, and a Tuesday, so when the door jingled five minutes after opening, I expected to see Wally lumbering toward me at the circ desk, his five movies and flower in hand.

But it wasn't Wally.

It was Trina.

I gasped one short breath at the sight of her. She walked straight toward me at the circ desk, her eyes piercing as arrows, her shiny hair twisted in a perfect fishtail braid.

"Good morning." I had never been so relieved to hear Sonia's voice. She lowered a stack of books onto the return cart but didn't take her place behind the computer. I realized right away what she was doing. She was giving me a chance to show that I wouldn't let Trina get to me anymore, that I had turned the page.

I stepped up.

"Good morning," I echoed Sonia, smiled brightly, and looked straight through Trina as if she were nothing but a deserted cobweb, sticky but harmless.

Trina startled for a moment, then quickly turned her attention to Sonia, snubbing me, and answered, "Good morning."

I stood my ground behind the computer.

"I have to grab some things from the back, Jamie. Run the desk for me, would you?" Sonia briefly touched my shoulder, probably to show Trina exactly whose side she was on.

Trina's whole face fell.

"Can I help you with something?" I asked cordially, glancing at her, then at the screen, then back at her again. I put my hands on the keyboard to show her I had work to do.

Trina let out a short, hard breath. "No, forget it. I can do it myself." She started to walk away, toward the back room. "I just wanted to get some art books for my brother," she called over her shoulder to me. She was a bee, trying to sting.

"In the 700s, on the left." My voice sailed out of me and through the room, smooth and clear. And I actually knew the correct Dewey decimal section.

Trina didn't acknowledge me or say thank you, but I didn't expect her to.

Sonia returned to the desk. "Well done, my dear," she said, nodding.

"Thanks." I smiled, not even trying to hide how proud I was of myself. "I Sonia-ed it."

"Excuse me?"

"I Sonia-ed it. I worked my inner Sonia and nailed it." I raised my eyebrows and grinned big. "Thank you for being so awesome, and for letting me copy your awesomeness."

"My awesomeness," Sonia repeated. "Well, I won't argue with that, Jamie. You're very welcome."

The bells rang as the door swung open, and a Wally shape filled the doorway.

"Good morning to you, and a good morning—" Wally didn't finish his greeting. He leaned against the doorframe instead and stood in place for a few breaths.

". . . it is!" I finished for him.

He nodded yes and lifted a hand to acknowledge me, but held his gaze down on the ground. Then he pushed off the wall and slowly worked his way to the front desk. He rested both arms on the counter once he got there. His eyes were dull and his face was coated with a thick layer of sweat.

"Hiya, Jamie," he managed to huff, extremely out of breath.

"Hey, Wally," I said, in a softer voice this time. "You okay?"

"Just tired today, a little short in my chest is all." He forced a half smile, then started his walk around the desk to his vase.

"Do me a favor and pull that old stem out of there for me," he directed, breathing heavily the whole time.

"Of course." I didn't offer it to him to take home, and he didn't ask for it.

Wally kept one hand on the counter while he searched with the other in his tattered plastic bag. He came out with a bloodred carnation. From a distance, it almost looked like a rose. Wally lifted his arm to slip it into the mouth of the vase and completely missed. It fell onto the counter and then dropped to the floor.

"I'll get it!" I nearly shouted, rushing from behind the desk to retrieve it before Wally could even consider bending down for it himself.

"I've got it, Wally," I told him, and I placed it in the glass jar. "It needs fresh water again. I'll take care of it. Can I check in your movies for you?" I reached for his bag without asking, something I had never done before, and he let me. I noticed Trina had come back into the main room and was watching, studying Wally and me instead of the large art book in her hands.

Lenny came downstairs from the loft, finished with fiction shelving for the moment.

"Good morning, Wally, my man," Lenny greeted him. "Shopping for some movies, I'm guessing?"

Wally smiled a genuine smile then, returning a bit to himself, and answered, "You know my routine. Gotta stick to my routine." He smiled a big, yellow-toothed smile. Even the gaps in his teeth smiled.

"Let me get you a chair. You feeling all right?" Lenny swung a chair from a computer station over to the DVD wall, blocking the aisle in that way Beverly allowed for Wally but nobody else.

"Not great, actually. Not so good. But not so bad, either." He perked up with his last words and mustered a laugh, as if he'd just told the punch line to a great joke. His laugh turned into a cough, of course, and Lenny grabbed him by the elbow to steady him as the cough rattled his body.

Lenny got Wally set up in his chair so he could search the DVD display, while Sonia and I returned to the front desk.

"Let me know if I can help you with anything, Wally," Lenny told him. Then he walked to the desk to tell Sonia he'd be downstairs in the supply closet if we needed him.

After Sonia renewed books for one patron and then helped an older woman with a reference question, she turned to me. Her face was tense.

"His color is off," she said. "He needs a doctor."

"Lenny tried that already. He wouldn't go," I reminded her.

"We have to try again." She looked back at him. He was seated, his hands on his knees, his round belly resting in his lap. I watched a drop of sweat trickle off his earlobe and land on his thigh like a tear. He didn't seem to feel it.

And then it all happened so fast.

His whole body slumped down into itself like a deflating balloon, and he collapsed out of the chair and onto the floor.

I saw the whole thing as if it were screened in slow motion, even though it must have been only one second from the beginning to the end of his fall.

"Sonia!" I shrieked as I ran toward the lump on the floor that was Wally.

Beverly appeared out of her office in a flash and seemed to teleport to the closest phone. She dialed 911, gave all the information in a clear calm voice, hung up, then wedged open the front door for the ambulance's arrival.

Meanwhile, Sonia met me on the other side of Wally.

"Roll him, Jamie, on his side, this way," she said, and started to push.

Lenny flew up the stairs and pushed in next to Sonia, helping to move Wally into position. He felt for a pulse. "It's there, but it's barely there," he told us, a tremor of fear in his voice.

A mixture of dried spittle and fresh saliva pooled onto the carpet beside Wally's mouth. It looked frothy. His eyes rolled back in their sockets.

I felt my throat close up and an icy sweat break out across my body. I moved the chair out of the way, pushing it into the room behind me, which was when I saw Trina, standing there, eyes wide, mouth open, frozen in place. The book she had been holding was splayed open at her feet, pages folded over themselves, the spine bent from hitting the floor.

"Please clear the entrance area," Beverly called out to all the patrons in the library. "If you could all just come to this side, please." She directed the small crowd to Black Hat Guy's side of the library. His quotes chair was empty, but no one sat down. No one sat anywhere. Many of them strained to see Wally's limp body, exposed and vulnerable on the worn carpet floor, then turned their backs and looked out the window instead, their hands over their mouths in shock.

"It's coming. The ambulance! I hear it!" one of the patrons by the window called.

"Please keep the front clear," Beverly repeated in a loud, calm voice.

Trina hadn't blinked. She started to sway on her feet.

Lenny looked up then and spotted Trina. "That girl's about to faint," he said to me. "Jamie, go," he ordered, his voice pained.

"Trina?" I called.

She didn't move. Her eyes were glued to Wally on the floor, to Lenny leaning over him, feeling for a pulse, listening for his breath.

"Trina!" I tried again.

Nothing.

I left Wally, grabbed her by the shoulders, and pushed her

through the other back room doorway and into the children's room. It was completely empty. I moved a chair over so it was facing the window and forced her to sit. Her skin had passed white and was becoming translucent. Her eyes fluttered. I unlatched the window in front of her and threw it open, even though the air-conditioning was running.

"Stay here, Trina," I directed her. "Everything's going to be okay."

I heard the EMTs bang through the front door with their stretcher.

I turned back to Trina. "The ambulance is here. Just look out the window and take deep breaths."

She stared out the window, but I don't know what she saw, if she saw anything at all.

"I'll be right back. Don't move."

She blinked once, then let her eyes close.

I stepped back into the main room, but the spot on the ground where Wally had fallen was empty. He was already on the stretcher, being rolled out of the library.

And then I saw it, pushed up against the bottom of the DVD shelf: his wallet. It must have fallen out of his pocket, or that awful ragged plastic bag, when he fell or when we rolled him or when they moved him onto the stretcher. The wallet was weathered and cracked and busting at the seams, much like Wally himself.

"Wait!" I yelled, to no one and everyone at the same time.

Lenny ran to me, took the wallet from my hand, and rushed it to Beverly, who was following the EMTs out the door, a paper fresh from the printer in her hand.

Then he returned to Sonia and held her while she silently wept into his chest. Several patrons whispered quietly to each other, a few returned to their workstations, most packed up and left.

I went back to the children's room. Trina was exactly where I'd left her.

"Wally's going to the hospital now. He's going to be fine." I said it because I wanted it to be true.

Trina turned and looked at me for the first time. She moved her head slowly, from side to side, as if she were telling me no, that he wouldn't be fine at all.

I noticed her cell phone, bedazzled in its pink rhinestone case, sticking out of her pocket, so I helped myself to it. I hit Favorites and tapped her Home setting. "I'm calling your mom. She'll come get you. Don't worry."

The phone rang twice and then someone answered.

A voice I knew, a voice I hadn't heard in weeks, said, "Trina?"

Trey.

I paused for half a second and then I said, "No, it's Jamie. At the library."

It was his turn to pause. "Jamie?"

"Yes." I barreled ahead, "Something happened here at the library, and Trina's upset." I was quick to add, "Nothing happened to Trina. She's fine. She just needs your mom to come get her. She can't walk home like this."

"Like what? What happened?" Trey's voice was soft and concerned. He was probably a great brother. Better than Trina deserved. No, that wasn't it. Jane Eyre wouldn't think that way, and Sonia wouldn't want me to think that way, either. Maybe Trey was better because that's what Trina needed, so she could become better herself.

"Someone collapsed, one of our regulars. An ambulance came. Trina saw it happen." I looked at Trina then. She was staring at me, the color trying to return to her face, the tight grip she had on the chair trying to relax. I turned away from her and told Trey, "She's pretty upset. Someone should come pick her up."

"Okay. I'll tell my mom. We'll be right there."

"Thanks."

"Can I talk to her?" Trey asked just as I was about to hang up.

"Hold on." I held the phone out to Trina. "Your brother wants to talk to you."

Trina stared at the phone in my outstretched hand, then looked at me, then back at the phone. Her mind was working, you could practically see it, neurons leaping and connecting behind her frightened eyes, but she still couldn't manage a word. She closed her eyes again.

I put the phone back to my ear. "Trey, she can't. Someone needs to get here."

"Okay, I'm coming right now." He hung up, but not before I could hear the beginning of his yell, "Mo-om."

I put Trina's phone on the seat beside her. "They're on their way."

A breeze of cool air pushed through the open window in front of Trina, smoothing back the hairs that had come loose from her braid. A second gust of wind followed the first, and Trina's chest rose as she took it in.

"Jamie, we were looking for you." It was Lenny, with Sonia a step behind him. He was holding her hand. They hurried over to me and gave me a joint hug.

"Are you all right?" Sonia asked, her eyes puffy from crying. She held me by the shoulders and backed up so she could get a look at all of me, like she was checking to make sure I was still in one solid piece.

"Yeah. Yes. I'm all right," I said. My eyes started to well up at the question, but I pushed the tears away. I shivered with the cold of my dried sweat, the adrenaline rush now gone, leaving me clammy.

"It's okay if you're not," Lenny assured me.

"I know." I hugged my arms against my stomach. "I just want him to be okay."

"We all do," Lenny answered. "Beverly went with him."

"She did?"

"She was great," Sonia said. "She even thought to print out his patron registration so she'd have all his information."

"I guess they'll call his kids," Lenny said, "at the hospital."

"They better show up this time," Sonia said, an edge to her voice.

"It's good you spotted the wallet, Jamie," Lenny told me. "You did good. With everything."

The tears started to form again. I could feel them, tiny prickles of heat collecting in my eyes. I blinked hard to crush them.

"And how about you, miss?" Lenny asked, releasing Sonia and squatting down next to Trina in her chair. "Are you all right?"

Trina gazed into his eyes and nodded yes.

"I'm sure you weren't expecting that when you came to the library this morning. That was scary."

"Uh-huh," she whispered.

Sonia was right. Everyone talked to Lenny.

"You've got this, Jamie?" Lenny mouthed at me quietly as

he stood back up to his skyscraper height.

"Yes." I nodded. "Her mom's on the way, so you can just send her back here when she arrives."

"Will do," Lenny said.

Sonia smiled at me, approval all over her face.

I smiled back.

Lenny filled his chest with air and then let it out slowly, like a deep meditative breath. The whole room seemed to relax.

"So, one of us should be at the front desk," I pointed out. "I'll stay with her."

"Of course," Lenny agreed. "I'll go."

"I'll go, too," Sonia said.

Lenny reached out and gave my arm a squeeze. Then they walked out together.

Trina sat in her chair, still as a mannequin, while I stood beside her, the two of us waiting together for her mom. Neither of us said a word. I gazed out the window and studied the scene before me so I wouldn't think about Wally. I saw a bright blue mailbox bolted to the sidewalk halfway up the block. Beside that was a wooden lamppost, leaning slightly, black wires both thick and thin hanging from it. Beyond that was a gingko tree full of fan-shaped leaves and small golden fruit growing from a stamp-size green space across the street. If Trey were sitting here, he would draw. He would pull out his sketchbook and pencils and lean over the page, then flick his head to move his long, dark bangs out of his eyes and draw.

Minutes passed and then there were fast footsteps, the *click-snap* of heeled flip-flops on the move, and Mrs. Evans appeared.

"Trina?"

Trina turned in her seat to meet her mom's eyes. In half a second or less, tears waterfalled down Trina's face and Mrs. Evans had her wrapped so tight in her arms you couldn't tell where one of them stopped and the other started.

"Oh, honey," her mom crooned. "Shh, it's okay."

Mrs. Evans rocked her daughter and stroked her hair and whispered in her ear while Trina cried.

I averted my eyes, turned, and zipped quickly out of the children's room.

Right into Trey.

I was only one step from knocking into him when I realized and slammed on the brakes.

We both took a step back.

"Hey," he said. His long brown bangs hung messily over his forehead, blocking one eye. He needed a haircut, but he looked great needing a haircut.

"Hey."

"She's in there?" he asked about the room behind me.

I nodded. "Your mom has her."

"Okay." He tossed his head a smidge to the left to move his hair back.

"Okay," I repeated, because I didn't know what else to say. Because of his eyes.

I got stuck in his eyes. Still! Stuck in the warm, deep-brown shine of them.

"She's really upset about what she saw," I said, to stop myself from gawking at him.

"It's because of our grandpop. She was there when he died. It was really sudden, like this," Trey explained.

"Wally didn't die," I said quickly. "They're helping him right now, at the hospital."

"That's good. For Wally—I'm glad. But they couldn't save our grandpop."

"I'm sorry," I said, my voice quiet.

"Trina was nine and we were at his house. She always liked to play in his study while he read his magazines—he had a huge rolltop desk with all these tiny compartments she loved. He got up to get a magazine off the shelf and that was it—he just had a stroke and collapsed, and Trina was the only one in the room with him when it happened. She started screaming like crazy and my parents ran in and found him on the ground and her on top of the desk, wailing. It was awful. They kept me out of the room, so I never saw anything except the ambulance arriving and leaving, but she saw it all."

I watched Trey look into the children's room then. Mrs. Evans was tucking hair behind Trina's ear while they stood by the window, talking quietly. Trina looked a hundred times better already.

Trey looked back at me and said, "She had nightmares for a while after that. She even started sleeping in my parents' bed for a while." He paused then and gave a half smile. "She'd kill me if she knew I told you that."

"I won't say anything," I hurried to tell him.

"I know you won't," he said. He stuck a hand in his back pocket, looked at the floor for a second, then lifted his eyes back to my face and said, "I trust you."

My breath caught in my throat, and then I had to look away, at the floor, at the lights, at the window in the next room, to collect myself.

"I also wanted to tell you—" He paused.

I looked back up at him and took a slow, deep breath.

"That I'm sorry." He shrugged one shoulder, just one, and kind of stuttered, "You know, about—"

"You don't have anything to be sorry for," I told him, my voice surprisingly steady and even and sure.

"Well, I wanted you to know that I'm not mad or anything.

I get that you were just trying to . . ." His voice trailed off, and then he said, "I really liked your letter."

I blushed immediately but didn't care. It was way too late to care about that. "I'm sorry if I embarrassed you."

"*I'm* sorry my sister embarrassed *you*. She shouldn't have done that. She just doesn't think things through sometimes, you know?"

"Actually, yeah, I kind of know all about that," I said, completely deadpan, which made Trey grin with his whole entire beautiful face. Maybe Trina and I had more in common than I thought, both of us acting quickly, stupidly, to get what we wanted. For me, it was to get closer to Trey. For Trina, I wasn't sure. Attention? Popularity? Approval? Only she knew exactly what she was trying to win.

"Well, still. I'm sorry how it turned out." And he glanced around him at the room, the shelves, the computers, the whole library.

And then I did something I never in a million years thought I could do when thinking about my colossal mistake back in May.

I smiled.

"I'm not," I said.

"You're not . . . what?"

"Not sorry about how it turned out." And then I did what

he did. I looked around me, at the circ desk and the shelves, at the furniture and the people, at this place that had been my home away from home all summer long. This place that had given me myself back, only better. A new and improved version of me.

"I'm sorry if I got you in any kind of trouble, but I'm not sorry how it turned out. At all."

He tilted his head and looked at me then. I could tell he didn't know exactly what to make of me, not just yet, but he was trying. And I liked that. A lot.

What he said was, "Thanks for taking care of my sister."

"You're welcome," I said back, and then took the staff stairway down to the kitchen. I pulled out my phone and dialed my mom's work number. While it rang, I thought about the morning, all that had happened between the time we opened and now. My heart fluttered in my chest. I pulled up a chair and lowered myself into it, rested my elbows on the table, and took a huge breath, hoping to wash everything scared and shaky out of me.

She answered on the fourth ring, right before voice mail picked up.

"Mom, it's me."

"Hi, Jamie. What's up?" A short pause, then, "You sound funny."

"I do?"

"You sound the way you do when you're trying to act like everything is fine but everything is really not fine."

"How do you do that?"

"I'm your mom. I live and breathe you."

"That's super creepy, Mom."

"Too bad," she said, and I could hear her smile. "Talk to me."

Her voice was comfort and hugs and movies on the couch together, a security blanket, even over the phone.

So I did. I told her everything.

Because sometimes you just needed to talk.

Beverly

→≫·≪←

The text buzzed through the next morning when I was still at home making my bed.

It was Beverly, about Wally.

He didn't make it.

Massive stroke.

Beverly wanted me to know before I came to work so I'd have a chance to process it on my own, in private. She said it was a terrible loss, but we still had a library to run. To save.

I hugged the thin blanket I was folding against my face and tried to push all my sadness into it.

Wally. Our Tuesday regular, our movie fanatic. Gone. We knew he was old, and you could tell from the coughing that he wasn't 100 percent healthy. But still.

I could already feel how much I would miss him. How

much we all would. Tuesday mornings at the library would feel strange now, off-balance, for a very long time.

I finished making my bed, splashed cold water on my face, and touched up the little bit of makeup I had just splotched with my tears. Then I locked the door behind me and headed to the library.

It was on my walk there that I remembered the window in the children's room, the one I opened for Trina. I'd never closed it! Everything was so crazy after Wally's ambulance exit. Beverly didn't even come back to the library that day, which was completely shocking to me but didn't seem to faze Sonia or Lenny at all, as if they knew something I didn't. We fielded a ton of questions all day at the circ desk as the news spread through town and people stopped in to find out who, what, when, but mostly who. We were all way too distracted to notice an open window in the children's room.

But that open window meant anyone could have climbed into the library overnight and grabbed any book, movie, or magazine they wanted, not to mention the cash we kept in the drawer for fines. Not to mention all the computer equipment. The whole library could have been ransacked.

And it would be all my fault.

Another colossal mistake.

Panic began to expand in my gut, and I felt suddenly

queasy. I stopped walking and leaned against a tree growing on the strip of green between the street and the sidewalk. I took a deep breath, and then an even deeper one.

The window was a mistake, but it was an honest mistake. It happened because I was helping someone who really needed help. This should be one of those mistakes that was easily forgiven. This should be one of those mistakes that wasn't followed by a punishment. Or *consequences*.

"It's not so bad," I told myself out loud. "It'll be okay." I picked up my pace and hurried to the library.

Everyone was already there when I arrived: Beverly, Sonia, Lenny, a bunch of regulars, plus a mom with a double stroller browsing the parenting magazines. And everyone was busy, doing their regular library things, like they had the day before and like they would the day after.

Like Wally never would again.

I hustled to the children's room and found the window the way I had left it, still open. I surveyed the room. Everything looked fine. The shelves were full, the toys were stacked in their buckets, the tablets were resting on the low tables waiting for small hands. Nothing was missing or broken.

I shut the window and locked it, relief flooding my body. I exhaled deeply and scanned the room again. When my eyes reached the doorway, I saw Beverly on the other side, looking at me.

Her eyes darted to the window I had just closed and then back to me, and she nodded. She knew. And she wasn't mad. I nodded back to her, and then she stepped away.

I filled a few empty display stands with picture books, straightened the puppets on their rack, and then went back to the main room.

And that's when I saw Wally's flower. The red carnation. The water had been changed.

"We should get a better vase," Beverly said quietly from behind me.

"Yes," I agreed, "we should."

But then I changed my mind. "Or not, actually. I think I like that little glass jar. It's so . . ."

Beverly finished my thought for me. "Wally?"

"Yes," I said, and I couldn't help smiling. "It's so exactly Wally."

"You were a great help yesterday, with everything. Thank you for that," Beverly told me.

"Sure." It felt weird to accept a thank-you when all I did was react. I didn't think at all; I just did.

And we still lost him.

"You could have taken today off, if you wanted to."

"I'd rather be here," I said.

Beverly nodded in shared understanding. "Yes, well, me too." She smoothed down the sides of her khaki pants with her hands, then clasped them in front of her. "I wanted you to know that I received a call from a patron's mother. A Mrs. Gabrielle Evans. She wanted to pass on her gratitude at how the library staff handled her daughter."

"Trina?" I asked.

"Yes, Trina." Beverly nodded. "I told Mrs. Evans that it was all you, that you took it upon yourself to help her daughter."

"What'd she say?" I shouldn't have asked but couldn't help it. I was sure Mrs. Evans had despised me from the moment she learned I was the one who'd planted the book on Trey.

"She sounded very grateful, Jamie. She said she'd be sending a card to the library to personally thank you."

"She's going to thank the boy-crazy kid who put her son in the middle of a cheating scandal?"

"No, Jamie." Beverly shook her head at me. "She's going to thank the compassionate kid who helped her daughter through a traumatic experience."

When she said it like that, it *did* sound pretty impressive.

Beverly placed her hand on my shoulder and declared, "'To err is human, to forgive, divine.'"

"You got that from the chair," I called her out, looking across the library toward Black Hat Guy's special seat, empty and waiting for him.

"Well, the chair got it from a writer named Alexander

Pope," Beverly replied, "but we'll have to save our discussion of eighteenth-century poets for a later date. There's a lot to catch up on today."

She gave my shoulder a light squeeze, then walked away, smiling and nodding at several patrons on her way back to her office.

My chest filled with a tingly lightness as I walked to the circulation desk. This was the exact opposite, in every possible way, of how I'd felt the day I was called out of the lunchroom and into the principal's office back in May.

Lenny and Sonia worked side by side at the circ desk, small Sonia with her usual cup of coffee and contagious energy, and tall Lenny with his shaggy gray ponytail and easygoing nature.

I arranged the newspapers, straightened the magazines, and then went outside to hit the book drops. I grabbed two bags but knew it would still be several trips, since I hadn't checked them at all yesterday.

As I rounded the library and reached the back, I saw a bright red cardinal on top of the audiobook drop. He was round with a full belly, red as Wally's carnation, and repeated his whistle-call several times. I could see the tiny muscles move in his neck and ripple down his feathered chest as he sang.

Shady was there too, curled up between the two book drops in the shade, head lifted and nose sniffing at the air. He clomped out of his space, climbed his front legs partway up the side of the container, and barked one loud, short, flat bark.

The cardinal took off.

I watched it cross the parking lot in the air and disappear behind another building. Shady watched it fly away, too, barking a few more *good riddance* yips as it went.

"Very friendly of you, Shady." I shook my head at him.

Shady trotted over to me and lifted his front paws up onto my legs. I let him sniff my library bags while I scratched him under his chin.

Shady looked different. His eyes were shiny and his fur was clean and smooth, detangled and brushed free of all the grit and dirt that usually clung to him. There was a lumpy cloth bed shoved deep between the drops, right where they backed up to the dogwood bushes. It was black and soft and was already dusted with a fine layer of Shady fur. One of his food bowls was licked clean and the other was full of water.

"Looks like the dog fairy has been visiting you," I told him, rubbing his back and side. He rolled over when I got to his hip, and his leg started pedaling furiously in the air as I scratched the same spot over and over.

"Well, that's just embarrassing," I told him. I scratched him another full minute and then patted his head. "All done now. I've got to empty these things. I'll check on you again later today."

It took three trips to empty the drops, and each time I came back, Shady looked up at me, practically smiled, and watched me work until I stepped away again.

Back inside, Sonia checked in the items and then passed them to me to double-check.

When the phone rang, she gestured at me to answer it.

It was a reporter from the *Biweekly*. They wanted an interview with Beverly about yesterday's incident. I winced at the word *incident*. How could they sum up a person, a Wally, and his forever death, as an *incident*? I put the reporter on hold.

"Sonia, it's someone from the paper. They want to talk to Beverly. How do I transfer the call?"

"Oh, no, Jamie. Don't transfer it. I'll take it," she said quickly, and reached for the phone.

"But they asked for the director," I said.

"No, I'll do it. She shouldn't have to." Sonia was sure. "Not about this."

"Why not?"

"Because it's"—she searched for words—"it's too hard for her."

"Because of Wally?"

"No, Jamie." She looked like she was done, but then decided to tell me, "Because of her sister."

I shook my head, still gripping the receiver against my chest. "I don't understand."

219

"Let me take the call and I'll explain after," Sonia said, reaching for the phone again.

"No. It's just a reporter. She can wait. What's going on with her sister?" I demanded, my voice shaking the tiniest bit.

"Beverly lost her sister. Years ago. Unexpectedly."

My mouth fell open, slowly at first, then all at once.

"It was a car accident, when they were younger. The accident was covered in all the papers and it was on the news and Beverly was hounded by reporters with tons of questions and, I don't know, it was really terrible for her. She won't even talk about it."

The sister she played library with, the sister I'd asked about being a librarian now.

"How do you know—"

"Lenny, of course. At some point she told Lenny."

Everyone talks to Lenny, I heard in my head.

"She didn't tell him much. He looked it up after and found the articles. The reporters were relentless with Beverly. There was even an editorial about that, about how some of them mistreated her just to get their scoop."

I let my body drop onto the stool behind me. "She used to play library with her sister, when they were little," I said. The image of it filled my head: the tea table, the rows of books, the stamp with no ink.

Sonia seemed to be picturing it, too. Then she told me, "They were walking home together and a car came right up onto the sidewalk and hit her. That was it. If it had been another foot over, Beverly would have been hit, too."

"But why?" I asked, unwilling to accept that explanation. "How?"

"A DUI."

"Driving under the influence?"

"Yes," Sonia said, anger and despair both tied up in that one word. "Drunk driver."

"Oh my God."

"So I'll take the call for her. I can at least do that," Sonia said.

Her very own sister.

Standing right next to her.

I handed Sonia the phone. She held her hand over the mouthpiece and took a deep breath.

"I can't believe it," I said to myself. Poor Beverly. No wonder she'd gone pale when I'd asked if her sister was a librarian like her.

My shoulders drooped even more and I stared at the square tiles on the floor. They were one foot wide. One foot more this way, I thought, and Beverly would have been hurt, too, maybe killed. Two feet more that way, and maybe her sister would still be here today. Such a small amount of space making such a big difference—it was mind-blowing to think about.

"That's beyond sad," I said, looking at Sonia, my eyes pleading. I wanted her to say something, anything, to make me feel better.

But she didn't.

"Sad doesn't even begin to cover it," she answered. Then she took the reporter's call.

Black Hat Guy

→→→·←←←

I couldn't help but stare when Black Hat Guy bounced into the library that afternoon at exactly 4:05. It was because I could see skin.

His heavy black sweatshirt was gone. He wore his same winter hat and rugged jeans, but his top half was draped in a baggy peach-colored T-shirt.

And I was pretty sure I knew where his sweatshirt had gone.

Black Hat Guy walked right back to the nonfiction stacks, found his dog book, and returned to his chair. He plugged in his phone, pulled a pen and a small spiral notebook out of his backpack, opened his book, and began reading.

Sonia was working the circ desk. She was off today, fidgety in a weird way. She had already dropped a home decorating book, which was so heavy it practically sounded like thunder when it hit the ground. She also dropped a DVD case, which opened on impact and sent the silver disc rolling in circles on the floor. She used her foot to stop it, clamping it with her wedge espadrille like a bug you wanted to trap but not squish all over the bottom of your shoe.

Sonia was a wreck because Beverly was meeting with Mayor Trippley at town hall, presenting our case to keep the library. Beverly had done her research and was very prepared. I knew because she practiced her speech on Lenny and me. She showed us charts of services provided and graphs of patron traffic by the hour, and even a list of other possible ways to address town budget issues.

Beverly was on Operation Save Library, and I knew she would succeed.

I guessed Sonia wasn't so sure, though.

I guessed Sonia was stuck thinking about what would happen if Beverly didn't succeed, about what would happen if the library disappeared.

This library was everything to Sonia. She had started volunteering at the library when she was my age—because she *wanted* to, not because she *had* to. Then she started officially working at the library the day she turned sixteen and had been here ever since. Sonia knew the library like it was an extension of her own body. She knew every warped floorboard, every dent in the plaster walls, every book on the shelves. Sonia knew which bangs and clanks in the pipes could be ignored and which required a call to the plumber. Losing the library would be like losing a part of herself.

No wonder she was so nervous.

I looked over at Black Hat Guy resting in his special chair, charging his phone. Where would he go every afternoon if the library wasn't here for him?

And what about the people who came every day to use our computers and printer because they didn't have their own? What about all the parents and kids who came here for books and movies they wouldn't have access to otherwise?

And what would have happened to Wally? If he hadn't been at the library that Tuesday, would he have been home, alone, collapsed on the floor, for hours, maybe days, before someone found him?

I shook that thought out of my head.

Beverly was probably wrapping up her presentation at this exact moment, shaking the mayor's hand and thanking him for his willingness to do the right thing for the people of Foxfield. Beverly would save the library.

She had to.

The phone rang, and when Sonia reached to answer it, she

knocked the receiver off the cradle and onto the floor.

"Dios mío," Sonia cried under her breath.

Lenny swooped in and scooped the phone off the floor, took the call, and then directed Sonia downstairs for a break.

"There's a fresh pot of coffee, *decaf* coffee, brewing right now," he told her, his hands on her shoulders, "and some pretty spectacular chia-seed bars on the staff table waiting for you to try."

Sonia looked at him and let out a deep breath.

"Go ahead," Lenny encouraged her. "Take as long as you need. Jamie and I have everything covered up here, don't we, J?"

"Yep, we've got it," I told Sonia, and I smiled extra big to convince her.

Lenny manned the circ desk and I found myself drawn back to the bulletin board. I had just cleaned it but it was somehow a mess again, all the current notices I had hung in orderly rows covered by crookedly slapped-on papers: a violin performance at a nearby church, an open-mic night at a coffee shop, an advertisement for personal training, an apartment for rent.

And this: *Animal Welfare Organization seeking volunteers.*

I read the flyer.

The Animal Welfare Organization had a shelter a few miles away and was looking for people to help socialize the animals. Cats needed to be played with, brushed, and handled.

Dogs needed to be groomed, walked, and taught basic commands. The AWO would offer free training in exchange for a commitment of eight hours per week of volunteer service.

I pulled the flyer off the board, folded it in half, and tucked it under my arm while I cleared out the rest of the unapproved junk on the wall. When I was finished, I saw Black Hat Guy's chair empty, the book, notebook, and phone all waiting for his return. Probably a bathroom break.

Before I even thought it through all the way, I walked over to his chair and slid the folded paper inside his dog book, right where the pen was holding his page.

I took half a minute then to act like I was searching the bookshelf directly behind his chair, just for cover, then stepped away.

The bells jingled.

"Good afternoon, Jim," Lenny greeted the mailman as he hoisted a thick stack of mail onto the counter.

"How you doing, Lenny?" Jim answered back.

"Good, Jim. It's all good." Lenny offered his regular fist-bump move, and Jim met it with his right fist. "Just these going out today." Lenny handed him a few envelopes.

"All right." Jim stashed them into the bag strapped diagonally across his chest. "Have a good one," he said, and the bells jingled behind him as the door closed.

"Now that's a job I would really love," Lenny confided.

"Mailman?" I asked.

"Yep. If I got a walking town, I mean. I wouldn't want to spend my day in a truck driving house to house, but if I could be on foot . . ." Lenny's face got all dreamy. "Outside all day, breathing fresh air, getting exercise, seeing different people all day long."

"What about when it's freezing out? Or hailing and windy? That doesn't sound so great to me," I pointed out.

"If it's cold, you dress for it. Rain? Dress for it. There's gear for weather. That's not hard. Not a problem at all."

"You know what?" I could easily picture him in uniform, walking the sidewalks, house to house, shop to shop, delivering mail. "I could *totally* see you as a mailman."

"Me too. Totally." Lenny shrugged his shoulders back and straightened his posture to his towering height.

"Except you'd never finish your route," I added.

"What?"

"You would stop to talk to everybody and make a million friends. Everyone would wait for you by their mailbox and hit you with all their problems and invite you in for tea and you'd never get your route done. Ever. That would be your every day. Because you're so easy to talk to."

"Oh, stop with the flattery." Lenny fake-shoved me away,

acting bashful.

"It's true and you know it." I fake-shoved him back.

"Yeah." He dropped his shoulders and let out a dramatic sigh. "You're right. I'd be the worst mailman ever. Fired my first week. Scratch that idea."

"It's scratched. Besides, the library needs you more." I grinned at him.

"You're a peach, Jamie, you know that? A fresh organic peach," Lenny said. "Speaking of which, those chia-seed bars downstairs have organic peach in them, and peach nectar. You gotta try them. They're great. You have to like cinnamon, though. I misread 'teaspoon' as 'tablespoon.'"

"Oh God."

"It's okay. Cinnamon is good for you. It's medicinal."

Black Hat Guy returned to his chair then. He found the flyer inside his book, looked up and scanned the room in confusion, and then bent down over the paper and read it.

I watched him from the circ desk, peeking from behind a magazine I held in front of my face as cover.

"Very discreet," Lenny said under his breath, like he was not at all impressed with my undercover skills.

I would be as good a spy as Lenny would a mailman.

Then the bells jingled again and Beverly was there.

And she wasn't smiling.

"Where's the petition, Lenny?" she asked without even saying hello.

"I have it. Downstairs. In my bag," Lenny answered like a kid in trouble.

"Go get it," she ordered, then softened her voice a bit and added, "Please. We need it. Now."

Sonia hurried up the stairs then, not looking any more relaxed than she had when she went down. "What happened?" she asked Beverly.

"He didn't buy it. Trippley didn't buy any of it. Repairing this building is too expensive. Cutting the library solves his problem perfectly."

Sonia closed her eyes and slouched against the wall. Lenny moved to her quickly and put his arm around her.

"So we're going to create a bigger problem for him," Beverly explained. "He needs to know that if he takes the library from residents, he'll lose their votes. And he needs their votes two years from now, less than two years, actually, if he wants to stay mayor, so we'll force him to reconsider." Beverly nodded once. "It'll work."

Beverly didn't leave the meeting with the answer she wanted, but she still got something out of it—she figured out exactly who she was dealing with. And if you knew who you were dealing with, you'd know how to deal. You'd know how to play the game. Beverly was betting the mayor *would* do the right thing if it meant saving himself.

"Yes!" Lenny pumped his fist, like the challenge had energized him. "I am *so* all over this!"

Sonia still looked unsteady.

"Use your library hours today to go door to door, Lenny. I have to follow up on a few things in my office and then I'll join you," she said. "Sonia, Jamie, can you hold down the fort?"

Sonia nodded yes, pushed her hair behind her shoulders, and walked slowly back to the circ desk.

"It's pretty much the only thing I can do," I heard her mumble under her breath.

And I definitely saw her blink back tears.

Sonia

→→→·←←←

When I pushed through the library door the next morning, I found Sonia practically doing a tap dance behind the circ desk. She was bustling with energy, arms flying and hair bouncing.

Lenny stood to the side watching her, shaking his head and grinning his face off.

"Umm, Lenny, how much coffee has she had?" I asked worriedly.

"This is not the work of coffee," Sonia answered for him. "It is what happens after a good night's sleep and an adjustment of attitude!"

"She's had a mug full of optimism, I think, with her usual six mugs of coffee," Lenny said to me.

"Optimism, schmoptimism," Sonia tacked back. "There's

nothing a new day can't fix. You see"—and she pointed dramatically to Black Hat Guy's chair—"it's right there in black and white, clear as crystal." Sonia read it out loud, enunciating every word, "'Wait for the common sense of the morning.'"

"Which writer said that?" I asked.

"I have no idea, and it doesn't matter," Sonia answered immediately. "Yesterday the world was falling apart, but that was yesterday. I've turned the page. We are going to be fine. Better than fine. No one is going to take this library away!"

Lenny crossed his arms in front of his chest and leaned against the wall, never taking his eyes off Sonia. He was loving every second of her giddy performance.

"If you would be so kind," Sonia started, searching through a stack of today's newspapers piled on the counter, "I have something I'd like you to read. In the *Biweekly*."

Sonia found the paper and flipped to the Letters to the Editor section.

"Take a good long look at this!" She flapped the paper open and held it in front of my face like a mirror. "First column, on the bottom."

And there it was, under the heading *A Letter of Gratitude*:

Dear Foxfield Residents,

A community is only as strong as its members and

services. I am writing this letter to express my deepest

appreciation for the community of Foxfield, and in

particular, Foxfield's exemplary public library.

Just a few days ago, an unexpected and tragic

event unfolded in the library. My daughter witnessed an

emergency medical situation that thoroughly shocked and

frightened her, but because of the truly heroic individuals

at the library, she was never in any danger of her own. One

person in particular, Miss Jamie Bunn, took it upon herself

to ensure my daughter's well-being. Miss Bunn located our

contact information, called us to explain the situation, and

stayed by my daughter's side until help arrived. I cannot

thank Miss Bunn and the library staff enough for their

genuine concern, attentive care, and timely response when

faced with such a challenging and unprecedented event.

The professionalism and exceptional service provided

by our library makes me proud to be a Foxfield resident.

Our library is a town treasure and will always hold a special

place in my heart.

With my deepest gratitude,

Gabrielle Evans

When I finished reading it, my eyes shot right back to the
beginning and I read it again. Lenny grabbed his own copy

from the stack and read it, too.

"Oh my God," he said.

"This is amazing," I whispered to myself.

"This is AMAZING!" Lenny shouted.

"Shh," Sonia scolded him. "We're in a library."

"Can you believe this? I can't believe this," Lenny said, again with too much volume. "The timing couldn't be more perfect!"

"Lenny, hush down. You're in a library. You are in the exemplary Foxfield Library, which provides very professional and . . ." Sonia paused, trying to remember. "Let me see that, Jamie. What did it say again?"

I turned the paper for her.

"Oh yes," she continued, pointing with her finger at the print, "very professional and *exceptional* service. I think we should send Trippley a personal copy." Sonia took scissors out of the desk drawer and cut the letter out of the paper, making sure to keep the printed date at the bottom of the page attached. Then she pulled out some glue and construction paper and mounted the letter onto a bright red sheet so the article was framed.

"I'm using our largest mailer so I won't have to fold it," Sonia said.

"It looks good," I said when she held it up for us to see.

"Why'd you mount it on red, though?" Lenny wanted to know. "I would have gone with blue, to use Foxfield town colors."

"Red's a fighting color, querido," she said with a devilish grin. "And this is war."

Then she hunched over the envelope and wrote out the address to Mayor Trippley at town hall.

I raised my eyebrows at Lenny and he raised his right back at me.

"I wouldn't mess with her when she's in a fighting mood," Lenny told me.

"I wouldn't either," I agreed.

And then he leaned in close to me and whispered, "She called me *querido*."

"Yes, Lenny," I whispered back. "I heard her."

Lenny glowed.

Wally

→→→·←←←

It was Tuesday, August 15, and in just a couple more weeks I'd be back at school. Eighth grade was pulling me closer with each passing day, promising all new teachers and new classes and the huge safety net of summer separating me from my big mistake at the end of seventh grade. I could start fresh, focus on my classwork, reunite with Vic, even rejoin the Art Club, although I knew it would be different without Trey. He would be joining a new art club, the one at the high school, the one you had to apply and be accepted to, which he had.

I realized right then how much I missed Art Club. I missed sitting still and looking at something so long and hard that it eventually became something else to my eyes. I missed making lines on paper—dark, light, thick, thin—until what pushed out of my pencil matched what I saw in my mind and felt in my chest. Because that's what drawing was for me—a feeling that came from the inside out. That feeling was either tight and stiff and frustrated when it wasn't going well, or loose and cool and smooth as icing on cake when it was.

I missed drawing on Fridays.

And then I had an idea.

Maybe once school started again, I could come to the library each week to draw Wally's flower. I could make it a yearlong study to submit as part of my portfolio for the high school Art Club. I could buy a special journal, and each page would be a flower portrait. It would show my commitment to the work, and my growth in skill, and it would reveal the color pattern, if there was one, of the flowers Wally chose for his special vase each Tues—

Wait.

What was I thinking?

Wally was gone. He couldn't bring flowers anymore for the jar on the circ desk. In fact, the last one he brought, that bright red carnation, was two weeks old and way overdue to be changed. The only reason it was still in the vase, the petals curled at the edges and shriveled up, was because none of us had the heart to pull it.

I didn't want to think about that jar being empty.

As I approached the library, I saw Lenny and Black Hat

Guy standing by the book drops, talking under a cloudless sky. I couldn't see if Shady was there in his usual spot, and I didn't want to interrupt my errand to check. I walked quickly past the building, then up the side street that led to Foxfield's only grocery store.

A small display of cut flowers greeted me as I stepped through the automatic doors. There weren't a ton to pick from, but it didn't matter. I just wanted something cheerful and bright to help fill the void Wally had left.

A clerk from one of the registers eyed me suspiciously. There had been a lot of shoplifting recently at the store, all covered in the *Biweekly*. She didn't need to look at me like that, though. After what I had been through, I knew I would never steal anything again for the rest of my life.

The clerk approached me.

"Are you going to buy something?" she asked, not bothering to keep the snark out of her voice.

"I need a flower," I replied, still scanning my choices. "Just one."

"One stem?"

"Yes."

"Well, if it's just one you want, then you have to go with the roses. Everything else we sell as a bouquet." Her voice lost some edge as she settled into her regular sales pitch.

"The roses are here." She pointed to the three pots at the top of the display, each holding a different color. "Today we got yellow, that's for friendship; red, that's for love, of course; and orange, which we don't see here too often."

"What's orange stand for?"

"It says on the card orange is for enthusiasm and passion." She huffed a little then, as if maybe she thought the whole color symbolism thing was nonsense. "So they say."

Wally had passion for the library. Wally showed enthusiasm every single time he came in, even with his deteriorating health closing in on him from all sides. He had enthusiasm and passion for the movies he checked out every week and always returned on time. Orange was a good match for Wally.

"Okay, I'll take an orange one, please."

"One orange it is," she said, and lifted a stem out of the bucket.

After she rang me up, she handed over the rose and said, "Now, don't forget this stem's got thorns on it. You got to watch where you hold it or you'll prick your skin and bleed like the dickens."

Another way to use the word *dickens*. I smiled to myself and decided I would mention it to Beverly later.

"Thanks," I told the salesclerk. I turned to leave, then stopped and looked back at her. She was standing over the open till, fighting with the wrapper on a roll of pennies she needed to add to the drawer.

I cleared my throat to get her attention. "You always have roses on Tuesdays?"

"Usually, yeah. Unless something's wonky with delivery," she answered.

"Okay, thanks." As long as the flowers were there, and as long as I could get to the store before school on Tuesdays, I would keep it going. I would do my best to keep Wally's vase full, and I would draw each flower like a weekly diary entry. *Flowers for Wally* could be the title of my project.

I hurried to the library. Wally's vase needed to be cleaned. It needed some fresh water and one sunshiny-orange, passionate rose.

It was going to be a beautiful Tuesday.

Beverly

-»»·«««-

Later that day, I was seated in Beverly's office, a pile of oat-meal-cranberry-carob cookies in a tin on the desk in front of me. Her day calendar was completely full, with names and times and abbreviations for all the things she had to do. A very neat stack of papers sat on Beverly's chair, and everything else on her desk was lined up as tidily as usual, all edges perfectly parallel or perpendicular as if arranged with a ruler.

Beverly had asked me to wait for her while she finished up with Lenny in the reading room. She was helping him put together a flyer outlining why the library was so important. The mayor was pushing the argument that libraries were irrel-evant in the "age of technology" because everyone had access to the whole world from their home computers. But his argument didn't include all the people who were not tech savvy and all the people who didn't have personal computers, not to mention the people who didn't have homes! He wanted to send Foxfield residents to Waverly, which was five miles away, and pay a fee—"a *very reasonable* fee," he claimed—to use their services. But what if you couldn't drive or didn't have a car or didn't have the money to pay for a service that used to be free?

Mayor Trippley had to be stopped, and Lenny's petition was our best shot. It turned out people *listened* to Lenny, too. He knew everyone and was collecting signatures left and right, whether they were regular library patrons or not.

Today's oatmeal cookies were lumpy and chunky and looked a bit like those other nest cookies, but the smell of sugary cinnamon wafting off them alone was enough to make my mouth water. I didn't know what carob was—it looked like chocolate but it wasn't chocolate—but those cookies were seriously good.

"Sorry to keep you waiting, Jamie." Beverly swept in, rubbing her hands together before her and nodding at me. She had come to work with a new hairstyle that morning. It was still fire-engine red but was cropped closer to her scalp than before and stood out in all directions in thick tufts around her head. Her hair made me think of punk rock and medieval weaponry at the same time. And it definitely wasn't what you'd expect to see with her yellow polka-dotted blouse and beige loafers, but that was Beverly.

She moved the papers on her chair to the floor, took a seat behind the desk, and, noting the tin of cookies, said, "Oh, how lovely." She looked out her door toward Lenny and nodded at his back, then turned back to me and offered me one.

"I've had two already," I admitted. "They're really good."

"Well then." She opened a drawer at her side, pulled out a sheet of paper, and got right to it. "This is the form I'm supposed to submit to your principal confirming your community service hours."

I shifted in my seat.

"You have worked well beyond the hours assigned to you"—she nodded at me as she said this—"and have provided immeasurable service here. In short, you have far exceeded the requirements of your community service, and I am going to make sure your principal knows that."

A wave of relief swept through my body. It was officially over: the crime, the humiliation, the punishment, even the self-loathing. Officially over and done with for good.

A line from the quotes chair popped in my head: *It's no use going back to yesterday, because I was a different person then.* I knew this one—it was from *Alice's Adventures in Wonderland.* Alice survived her long fall down the rabbit hole and the mysteries she faced once she landed. I had survived my long fall and had turned it into something else altogether. I was a different person now.

Beverly smiled and signed the bottom of the time sheet in front of me.

"I will be mailing this back before school begins, in the next week or two, with a letter I will compose describing how you have exceeded all our expectations and became an essential member of staff this summer."

"Thank you, Beverly," I said, blushing at her praise.

"You're very welcome." She answered, then continued in her professional library director voice, "Please know I would like to extend your position here as a permanent volunteer and, if we are able to keep the library up and running, would love to offer you a legitimate part-time position once you are old enough. You can get working papers at fifteen or sixteen, I believe. And I will, somehow, find a way to obtain funding for your pay."

My eyes lit up. "Really? I would *love* to stay here, and then to have an actual real job here, like Sonia and Lenny—that would be amazing!"

"It would be amazing for all of us." Beverly smiled once but then quickly dropped her grin to say, "But, as you know, first we have to deal with—"

"The mayor," we said at the same time.

"How can he do this?" I pleaded. "Doesn't he know how many people rely on us, how much they need us? Doesn't he know how much we do for the whole town?"

"I think there are a lot of things the mayor knows and a lot of things he doesn't. I don't think he has any idea what kind of opposition he's about to face, for one thing," Beverly said with a smooth cool in her voice. "The letter from Mrs. Evans and the petition are strong arguments for our side. If he goes against residents' wishes, he won't be reelected. He knows that."

"So we just have to let him know what residents want," I finished.

"Exactly. And Lenny has been working tirelessly on that. I think he's surprised himself with how many names he's collected already."

I smiled in triumph and folded my arms across my chest as if it were all settled and done. But Beverly didn't look ready to celebrate. We hadn't won anything yet.

"There's one more thing," Beverly said, bending down to reach into the bottom drawer of her desk. She came back up with a book in her hand. It was an old paperback, the edges faded from sun, the binding fragile as a baby bird. She passed it to me. "I wanted to give you this. It was my very first copy. My sister Dorothy and I"—she swallowed, then relaxed her lips into a gentle smile—"we shared it, passed it back and forth like a bag of candy. Only better, because when we finished it, we could just begin again."

It was a copy of *Jane Eyre*.

And it was beautiful.

The cover illustration showed Jane in a long black cloak fastened at her neck over a heavy burgundy dress, her white-gloved hands resting on her bustled skirt in front of her. Thornfield Hall stood in the gray distance, surrounded by bare, scraggly trees, and several windows of the house were lit in an ominous shade of red. Approaching Jane on horseback was Mr. Rochester, his face in shadow, his mood unknowable. I had never seen this cover illustration before.

"Beverly, I can't—" I began, but she cut me off quickly.

"I want you to, Jamie, please." She was looking right at me now, telling me straight and true. "I would love for you to have this book. I would love for you to read it again and keep it always."

I picked the book up and felt both the lightness and weight of it in my hands. The book was thick and worn, and the page edges were soft as velvet against my skin. I clutched it to my chest. "I will. I'll keep it forever, I promise," I told her. "Thank you so much, Beverly. This is really special."

"Well, so are you. Thank you so much for joining us this summer." She reached up to the locket around her neck and fingered it, sliding it back and forth on the chain, then released it back down under her shirt.

And that's when I knew, clear as if I'd opened it and looked with my own two eyes, that it was her sister, Dorothy, tucked away in that locket. Beverly carried her sister to the library with her every day, nestled in gold above her heart.

"Would you like a few cookies before you go?" Beverly asked then as she heaved a huge stack of papers from the floor back onto her desk. She still had a library to run.

"I'll take some from the stash downstairs. I think Lenny made those for you to take home," I told her.

As I stepped out of her office, the entrance bells jingled and I saw Mrs. Evans march through the door. She scanned the library space and spotted Lenny just as he lifted his head from his laptop, smiled, and waved her over.

I knew then for absolute sure—Mrs. Evans had meant every single word she wrote in that letter to the *Biweekly*. She had officially joined our fight.

Lenny

→≫·≪←

"Jamie, you got a sec? I have something to show you."

It was Friday afternoon and Lenny was leaning over a table in the reading room, where he had been stationed all week, organizing flyer campaigns and collecting signatures for the petition.

I left the cart of audiobooks by the wall where I was shelving and met him by the magazines. "What's up?"

Lenny was looking at a drawing spread out on the table in front of him. I followed his gaze down to it.

"Whoa" came out of my mouth as an involuntary response.

It was amazing.

I stepped closer to look.

The drawing was done in a satiny black ink on a white background. It showed an open book with an adult fox and her baby fox on the left page, gazing at a barren field on the right. The words *Foxfield Library Friends League* were hand-printed in calligraphy. The words circled the book image, and so did a leafy vine that followed the path of the words, swirled beneath the two foxes, and ended with one thin tendril of vine taking root in the empty field. It took my breath away.

"Pretty incredible, huh?" Lenny asked me.

"It's gorgeous. What's it for?"

"We started a group." And he cleared his throat to recite, "Foxfield Library Friends League is a collective of dedicated library advocates who support the advancement of their local public library and the services it provides."

Then he raised his eyebrows at me. "Pretty impressive sounding, don't ya think?"

"We have a league now? Of supporters?"

"We sure do. Lots of libraries have volunteer groups who fund-raise and help them in different ways. We decided it was time we had one, too. And we have three volunteers who agreed to co-run the league for us and recruit members."

"This is so awesome!"

"And this is our official seal." He held up the paper, his arms stretched out long and straight before him so we could consider it from a distance. Lenny's arms were long enough that the drawing really *was* a decent distance away.

It was stunning, and it was ours.

"Who made it?" I wanted to know.

Lenny kept his eyes glued to the drawing and answered, "A local student by the name of Trey Evans."

I gulped.

Trey did this? For us?

"Trey Evans," I repeated. It was all I could say.

"The one and only," Lenny confirmed.

"But why?" I managed to get out. "I mean, how?"

"His mom. She's one of our biggest supporters." Lenny put the drawing back down on the table and carefully covered it with a protective sheet of tissue paper. "And that's all because of you." When he looked at me then, I saw the exhaustion in his face, the small swooshes of blue collecting under each eye. Between his two jobs and the library campaign, he had been working nonstop.

"It turns out Mrs. Evans has some pretty powerful friends in town, and she's been working them on our behalf," Lenny continued to explain. "And then she mentioned that her son was a great artist and would be happy to design a logo for the Friends League."

It was amazing the way everything had shifted gears in just a few months. That confusing quote from Black Hat Guy's chair ran through my head again: *Time changes everything except something within us which is always surprised by change.* That quote had bothered me all summer, literally stopping me in my tracks several times as I read it over and over, trying to understand it.

And now I thought I finally got it.

So much had changed in just a few months, and not just in the mess of me and Trey and Trina. The library, which I'd walked by hundreds of times without giving a second thought, was now my favorite place to be. Wally, who had made the library a regular part of his life, would never lean on the counter or borrow flicks again. Lenny and Sonia, who had worked side by side for years, were maybe, finally, growing into something more. Things change. We all knew this. But it still surprised us every time it happened. That was what the quote was saying.

I had forgiven myself. Mrs. Evans had forgiven me, too, and so had Trey.

"Trey's an amazing artist," I bragged for him, although I was really just stating the obvious.

"So now we have this great logo and Mrs. Evans knows someone willing to print up T-shirts for us. We're moving right along."

"What can I do to help? I want to do something!" I felt infused with energy, like a hummingbird after a hit of sugar water.

"Keep doing what you're doing," Lenny said in all sincerity. "You covering for me at the desk, and everywhere else, allows me to work on this and keep the momentum going. We need a tsunami of pressure as fast as we can whirl it up."

"I was hoping for a more exciting assignment than that," I said, slightly deflated. "But okay, I'll keep doing what I'm doing."

"Thanks, J. You're the best." Lenny clapped me on the shoulder as he said it.

My eyes fell on the drawing again, the strong ink lines pulsing through the thin tissue paper on top. "And I can't wait to get my T-shirt. Any way we can speed that up?"

"I was just about to call Mrs. Evans now," Lenny told me, picking up his cell phone. "I'll let you know."

Black Hat Guy

>>>·<<<

S onia and I both did a double take at the sight of Black Hat Guy strolling through the library entrance on Monday. We checked the clock above the door, then looked back at him again.

It was 11:13 in the morning.

And Black Hat Guy was here.

In the library.

Black Hat Guy dropped his stuff in the usual spot, then crossed to the other side of the circ desk and helped himself to a newspaper. He returned to his chair, sat with one ankle crossed over his knee, opened the paper with a firm snap, and disappeared behind it.

"Well," Sonia leaned in to tell me, "I don't know if that's a good sign or a bad sign, but it's a sign, all right."

"Of what?" I asked.

"Of something," Sonia said with an eerie hush in her voice.

I looked again at the clock—11:14—and then out the window at the calm blue morning sky.

"Well, now you're freaking me out," I said.

"He's in a different shirt, too. Did you see?"

"It's bright purple. Kind of hard to miss," I answered, although I couldn't see it at that moment. From where I stood, it looked like a pair of denim jeans had sprouted a huge page of newsprint.

Lenny came into the library then with three people I'd never seen before, a small pile of books cradled in his arms.

"Good morning, Jamie." He nodded at me, then slowed his pace to look at Sonia and nod in a whole different way as he greeted her. "Sonia," he said, and I don't know how he did it, but he managed to say her name like it was a line from the most romantic poem ever.

And Sonia blushed. You couldn't miss the rosy flush that flooded her neck and cheeks.

"For you from the book drop, Jamie. Thank you." Lenny slid the books onto the counter and then proceeded to the campaign area with his followers.

Black Hat Guy lowered his paper at the sound of Lenny's voice, but Lenny didn't look at that side of the library. He was on a petition mission.

Beverly appeared then suddenly, at the bottom of the loft

staircase, from one of her inspection rounds. I watched her shake hands with each of the people Lenny brought in, rubbing her hands up and down the sides of her pants between each one, which I hoped they didn't mistake as her rubbing off their touch. If they knew Beverly at all, they would know that was just one of her mannerisms, her nervous tic. I had learned over the summer that Beverly was a lot stronger than she looked, like that trick candle on a birthday cake that looked so easy to snuff out but instead left you breathless and winded, worried about your wish. Beverly was not one to be knocked out so easily.

Lenny showed his group the drawing Trey had made, while Beverly continued to nod and thank each person repeatedly for their support. Then she silent-stepped her way back to her office, and after a few more minutes, Lenny brought his petition to the circ desk.

"Look at this." He turned the papers to face us. "We've officially passed our goal for signatures. I had to print new sheets and I still have people coming in later today to sign."

Sonia squeezed Lenny's hand, and with the way he looked back at her, I almost felt like I should leave the room.

"So"—I cleared my throat—"when will you deliver the petition? When do you stop collecting?"

"Beverly will let me know." Lenny pulled himself out of

his Sonia trance. "She's been working another angle with some other library people she knows. It should be soon, though."

"My mom is coming by later today to sign," I told him.

"Terrific." Lenny pulled two blank sheets from his stack and attached them to a clipboard. "I'm leaving these sheets here so you can collect from anyone who comes in while I'm gone. I'm going door to door to the shops in town to see who we've missed."

"Okay, we're on it," Sonia said.

Black Hat Guy ruffled his newspaper forcefully and then gave it a hard shake as he worked to fold it back up. The paper didn't cooperate, but it got Lenny's attention.

"Hey, look at you there," Lenny said, "all bright and early."

Black Hat Guy stood up then as Lenny walked over. I read three large letters printed in white across the front of his shirt: *AWO.* Underneath was printed *Animal Welfare Organization Since 1959.*

"Yeah, well, I gotta be somewhere at noon and I won't be done till late and you'll be closed by then," Black Hat Guy explained to Lenny, but loud enough for all of us to hear.

"Nothing wrong, I hope?" Lenny asked, ready to console and counsel.

"Nah." Black Hat Guy shook off that notion, then half grinned as he said, "Got a gig, actually. I'll only make it here in the mornings from now on, if it's a keeper."

"Really?" Lenny clapped his hand on Black Hat Guy's shoulder and gave him a nudge. "Whereabouts?"

"Just over in Taunton, at the AWO." And with that he grasped the bottom edge of his shirt with both hands and tugged it out straight so Lenny could easily read the print.

"Not bad, man, not bad," Lenny said approvingly. "You're working there now?"

"Kind of." Black Hat Guy turned around to show Lenny the back of his shirt, which had the word *VOLUNTEER* stamped in white print right in the middle. He turned back around and explained, "Already did my training, and now I'm putting in my volunteer hours. Could turn into something, though, maybe." He shrugged and tilted his head like it was all out of his hands, but he couldn't hide the hopeful ring in his voice.

"Sounds promising. Good for you, man." Lenny reached out to shake his hand.

"Thanks." Black Hat Guy shrugged again and admitted, "Yeah, well, it turns out I'm pretty good with dogs."

"Oh yeah?" Lenny was so happy for him you could feel it from across the room.

"I just get them, I don't know," Black Hat Guy explained. "It's kind of natural to me, even with the tough ones." Then he paused a moment and added, "Especially with the tough ones.

Some of those dogs haven't been treated right, you know."

"You're doing a great thing," Lenny told him, his voice swelling with admiration. "A really great thing. I'm happy for you, man."

"Yeah, thanks," Black Hat Guy said. "So far, so good."

He returned to his seat and started scrolling through his phone, and Lenny checked in with Beverly before heading out to collect signatures in town.

Sonia took Wally's vase downstairs to refresh the water for the orange rose I bought last Tuesday, and I manned the circ desk, double-checking returned items before putting them in order on a shelving cart. I printed out guest passes for two different computer stations and was able to get both visitors to sign the petition.

An older woman in dark jeans and high-heeled flip-flops asked about the new Diane von Furstenberg book, so I walked her to the Biography stacks in the back room.

And staring out at me from the shelf, right at eye level, was a brand-new biography of Charlotte Brontë. The cover was a pinkish-red color with a drawing of Charlotte's face, and before I knew it, it was in my hands and I was reading the summary on the back. The book explained how the crush Charlotte had on a man in her own life inspired the love story she wrote in *Jane Eyre*. *I* had a crush in real life, *and* I had read *Jane Eyre*, so this book was practically made for me!

I had to read it.

The book was really fat, though, and when I flipped through the inside I saw that the print was tiny. It would probably take an entire summer for me to get through it, and summer was practically over. I already knew eighth grade came with a lot of homework. Plus Art Club. Plus volunteering at the library (if we still had a library) . . .

I guessed the Brontë biography would have to wait.

"Excuse me, ma'am." Black Hat Guy was waiting for me when I got back to the circ desk, his backpack on, his cell phone in the hand he was resting on the counter. His winter hat was pushed back so more forehead was visible than I had ever seen before. It made his eyes look larger and his face younger than it did when the hat was pulled down low over his eyebrows.

"Hi, yes?" I asked, surprised to be referred to as *ma'am.*

"You've got a petition going, I heard? For the library?" he asked.

"Um, yes, we do. It's right here." I slid the clipboard in front of him. "We've reached our goal but are still collecting more. You didn't sign yet?" I couldn't believe Lenny hadn't collected from all the regulars already.

"No, I was gonna, but I didn't get to it. I'll sign now."

"That'd be great, thank you." I handed him a pen and

pointed out the different spaces, "If you could print your name here, then sign here, and then put your address," I stumbled, but caught myself quickly, "or just some contact information here, that would be great." I kept my eyes on his shirt, focusing on the *AWO*, as he took the pen and began to write.

"You know, there was a dog hanging out behind the library, by the book drops, and he looked like a stray, but I haven't seen him lately," I mentioned.

"Yeah, I know about that guy. I took him into the shelter already, the AWO." And he motioned to his shirt then. "They cleaned him up and there's already two applications for him. He'll have a good home soon."

"Wow, that was fast," I said, pleased to know his scavenging days were over.

"The small dogs get adopted faster," Black Hat Guy explained to me. "At the shelter at least, that's what they say."

He finished writing and slid the clipboard back to me, placing the pen down on top of it. "You got a dog?" he asked.

"No. Nobody's home all day at my house. My mom said it wouldn't be fair to leave a dog alone all day."

"That's true," Black Hat Guy agreed. "Well, if you ever want to hang out with some dogs or walk one or play or something, come to the shelter. They like having visitors there, you know."

"I didn't know. Thanks. Maybe I will." This was my longest conversation ever with Black Hat Guy. In fact, this was my *only* conversation ever with Black Hat Guy. "I'd love to see Shady again before he gets adopted and leaves for good."

"Shady?"

I felt a shy smile creep onto my face. "That's what I named him. Because he always curled up between the book drops in the shade."

Black Hat Guy laughed. A short, sincere laugh.

"I like Shady. The shelter named him Snickers. Adopters usually give their own names, though. But I'll think of him as Shady now." Black Hat Guy smiled at me, and I smiled right back.

"Thank you for signing the petition," I said again.

"Well, can't let 'em close the library."

"No, we can't," I agreed.

He tipped his head at me then, waved with his cell phone hand, and left the library, the bells chiming a sweet note behind him.

Sonia returned with a fresh cup of coffee and Wally's vase, the water clear and the flower still standing tall. Roses seemed to last a lot longer than carnations.

"I got more signatures, Sonia." I showed her the paper with the newest additions.

"Excellent," she said, sipping her coffee and reading the

newest names. "Oh my God," she suddenly exclaimed. "You've got to be kidding me."

"What?" I asked, alarmed I might have done something wrong. I quickly explained, "Instead of an address, I said he could just put his contact information. He doesn't have an address, Lenny told me, but he should still be able to sign—"

"No," Sonia cut me off. "That's not it. Look at his name."

It hadn't occurred to me to read what he wrote or check his signature. To me he was Black Hat Guy—I forgot he had a real name.

I peered over Sonia's shoulder to see the last entry on the petition. And there it was, written in all capitals, neat as a computer font but with a pressure that left a deep indent on the page beneath.

In the name column he had printed: *Rusty Shine.*

"His name is Rusty Shine?" I asked.

"Wow." Sonia was incredulous. "How's that for a mixed message?"

"Jeez Louise," I said under my breath.

"Well, it's not as bad as that," Sonia riffed without missing a beat.

"Ha-ha." I smiled at her. "But seriously?"

"Seriously, Jamie," Sonia said, "Jeez Louise is a terrible name."

"So-nia," I complained, "come on."

"His is only slightly better," Sonia admitted.

"Rusty Shine," I said again. "That's a total oxymoron."

"It's oxy-confusing is what it is. What's a kid growing up with a name like that supposed to think?" Sonia asked.

Did Black Hat Guy grow up identifying with Rusty, something worn and old, damaged and dangerous to the touch, or did he just focus on Shine, like moonlight on the sea, or a bright, sparkling star? Maybe at different times in his life he had felt like each.

"Well, my last name is Bunn. That hasn't been so great," I told Sonia. "Kids used to call me Jamie *Bum*."

"Yes, but at least your parents didn't name you Hot Dog or Hamburger. Then you'd be Hot Dog Bunn or Hamburger Bunn." Sonia poked me, laughing at her own silliness.

"They could have named me Toasted and then I'd be Toasted Bunn."

"Or Sugar Bunn. Or Sticky Bunn. Let's make a list." Sonia grabbed a pen, but then the phone rang. She stuck her tongue out at the phone, then straightened herself back to her professional librarian stance. "Foxfield Public Library, can I help you?" she spoke into the phone just as she had hundreds, probably thousands, of times before.

I looked back at the last entry on the petition.

Rusty Shine.

His signature was not very different from his printed handwriting. He had listed his email under the address column as I suggested. I guessed that meant he still didn't have a permanent home. But maybe he would soon. Maybe his volunteer work would lead to a real job, which would lead to a home. Maybe he was on his way.

I pictured him at the animal shelter, training dogs, helping the neglected ones develop trust and become adoptable. Maybe he had just been stuck living the rusty part of his life the last few years, but now, things would turn around for him. Maybe his life was slowly righting itself, shifting to embrace the other part of his name, to claim everything that was positive and happy and good.

Maybe he was finally turning the page so he could shine.

Sonia

->>>·<<<-

Lenny returned to the library after lunch with two dozen more signatures and a gallon of fresh peach iced tea. Sonia and I gathered around his campaign table and we read over lists and stapled packets, sipping tea so cold and sweet it almost hurt my teeth.

We had enough signatures now to be a serious threat to Mayor Trippley. I knew it was too early to celebrate, and I knew I had a whole cart full of shelving to do, but I felt so hopeful and happy that I wanted to enjoy it for just a few more minutes before I got back to work.

And then he walked in.

A man wearing a dark suit and a very serious face walked into the library, right to the circulation desk. He was carrying a shiny black briefcase, so perfectly polished you could practically see your reflection in it.

Sonia left her cup of iced tea with Lenny and went behind the counter. I followed just a few steps behind her. She raised herself up to the fullest extent of her height behind the circ desk, lifting up on her toes a bit inside her already high-heeled shoes. Lenny stopped shuffling the papers he was working with and eyed the man cautiously. I went to the cart behind Sonia and started alphabetizing the returns. They were already in alphabetical order, but I continued fussing with them anyway. I couldn't just stand there doing nothing.

It was impossible not to feel nervous.

"Hello. May I help you?" Sonia greeted the man in the suit. Her jaw was just the tiniest bit clenched.

"Good afternoon, yes. I'm here to speak with the director of the library, please, a Ms. Beverly Cooper," the suit man said.

I noticed his jaw looked entirely relaxed.

"Of course. And you are?" Sonia asked as she picked up the phone, poised to dial Beverly's extension and give her a name before the man showed up at her office door.

"I'm Alan Stutler, from Stutler and Bowan. Here's my card." And he reached inside his suit jacket and presented a small white business card. I looked over Sonia's shoulder at the black print bearing the name he'd just announced, under which was printed *Attorneys-at-Law*. It was the world's most boring business card. He obviously hadn't had a talented son like Trey to consult when he designed that thing.

And then, as if on cue, Beverly appeared. She was probably about to do another round of inspections, checking the status of each room in the building, when she spotted the unfamiliar man at the front desk and silently walked over.

Sonia replaced the receiver on the phone and let out a defeated sigh.

Mr. Stutler immediately shifted his attention to the approaching Beverly.

"Hello there," Beverly welcomed him, nodding.

"Hello. My name is Alan Stutler from Stutler and Bowan. Might you be Beverly Cooper?" he asked.

"I am, yes," she answered, and clasped her hands in front of her.

Mr. Stutler reached inside his suit coat again and retrieved another identically dull business card and handed it to Beverly. "I was wondering if I might have a few minutes of your time?"

Beverly took the card, read it, looked up at Mr. Stutler and then back down at the card in her hand.

"Perhaps we should go to my office," she managed, and pointed the way, her hand gripping the business card like her life depended on it.

The door closed with a click behind them.

Lenny, Sonia, and I all exhaled at the exact same moment. Had we all been holding our breath that whole time?

"What's going on?" I asked.

Sonia didn't answer. She glanced back at the closed office door again, and then over at Lenny, who was slowly shaking his head, lips pursed together, completely puzzled.

"Lenny, you always know what's going on." I stated this fact as if he just needed the reminder and then he would be able to answer my question. "What's up?"

"He doesn't know," Sonia spoke for him. "We don't know, mami."

That was not what I wanted to hear. "W-well," I stuttered, trying to come up with something, some thought or idea that might be helpful, and failing.

So then I just asked, "What should we do?"

"There's nothing *to* do. We have to wait and see," Sonia sighed. "Lawyers are not always bad news, you know," she added hopefully.

Lenny lifted both hands to his head and ran them slowly through his long hair. I noticed a dried blob of tan paint on his thumb. He was so tired he probably didn't even realize it was there.

"I'm going through everything in my mind," he said. "I'm sure we've followed protocol. We haven't done anything that could get us in trouble." He paused, then pushed his chair back and stood up. "I just don't know what this could be about."

"It's okay," Sonia assured him. "Whatever it is, it'll be okay."

Lenny was usually the one consoling others. It was unsettling to see Lenny be the one who needed help.

The front door jingled and some regulars strolled in. They went through their usual routines by the new book shelving, the DVD wall, the newspaper rack, and the public computers.

Sonia signed up a new-to-town mom with library cards for herself and her two daughters. She put holds on a whole list of books for Bernice Yancey, who always came in with a handwritten list of titles her daughter-in-law had told her she *must* read. Sonia usually found them in large print, too, which Bernice loved. I worked on a display of new audiobooks and then shelved books and DVDs from yesterday's carts. Lenny worked on the library campaign on his laptop, looking up at the door every time the bells jingled to see if he could grab another signature for the petition.

When there was a lull in activity, Sonia motioned me to come over. She had her finger over her lips, hushing me so I'd come quietly. She peeked over her shoulder at Lenny, who was busily typing away, and then grabbed my shoulder and turned me forcefully so my back faced him.

"Oh my God, Sonia, what?"

"Shh, I have to show you something." She bent under the circ desk and pulled a rectangular Tupperware container out of the giant bag she carried to work every day. "Keep your back like this," she instructed me when I began to turn. "We're making a wall."

"O-kay," I whispered, and righted myself back into wall formation.

"Look what I did," Sonia said then, quietly lifting the lid off the container to reveal a pile of sugar cookies. "I baked them last night. I need you to try one and tell me what you think. And be honest," she ordered.

"Oh, they're birds. Cute." The cookies were shaped like songbirds in flight, short wings outstretched on each side and a pointed small beak tipped upward. There was a dab of shiny black icing for the eyes. "You made these?"

"Don't sound so surprised. Mateo and I used to bake a lot. When he was little, I had alphabet cookie cutters, and that's how he learned his ABC's. Smartest purchase I ever made, those cookie cutters."

"These look great," I told her, still feeling too nervous about the lawyer to actually enjoy eating one, though. He had been in the office with Beverly for a long time. The door was still closed and we couldn't hear a peep.

"I think they're pretty good, but I need you to tell me for

sure before I, you know, put them out for everyone." There was a sudden shyness to Sonia's voice and a little flush to her cheeks.

I glanced at Lenny, still focused on his screen, and then at Sonia, holding the cookies out for me. Since Lenny had been too busy to bake for Sonia, Sonia was baking for Lenny. I suddenly felt like I was back in second grade, delivering messages between two classmates who liked each other, except now the messages were cookies.

I bit a wing off one bird and was surprised at the combination of lemon and sweet that filled my mouth. The light citrus flavor calmed my stomach somehow, and I quickly took another bite.

"So you like them. They're good, right?" Sonia asked, a smile of relief creeping across her face.

"Mm-hmm," I answered, still chewing.

"I just thought of shredding some lemon zest in there at the end. It works, though, right?" Sonia was asking, even though she already knew the answer. *Fishing for compliments* was what my mom called this.

"They are *so* good," I told her. "I love the lemon. What else is in there? Are they healthy?"

"Healthy? No! Lenny does the fancy-schmancy healthy food. This is good old flour, sugar, and butter. And lemon. This is old school." Sonia put the lid back on the container and pulled a pretty basket lined with parchment paper out of her gigantic bag. "I'll take these downstairs and set them out on the table."

"Very cute—birds in the basket. It'll look like they're in a nest."

"That's why I used the bird shape! I know what I'm doing."

As Sonia started down the staircase to the kitchen, Beverly's office door swung open.

"I'll let myself out. Thank you again for your time." Mr. Stutler stood in the doorway, addressing Beverly. "I'll be in touch soon."

Mr. Stutler closed the door behind him and walked briskly to the front of the library. He bobbed his head at me behind the circulation desk and politely said, "Good day," without losing a step, then left the building.

I stared through the glass window on the door and watched him recede into the distance, his head fading away, becoming fuzzier by the second like the details of a bad dream.

I turned then toward Lenny, who was already staring back at me, the same question on his face that none of us knew the answer to.

Sonia did an about-face on the stairs, still holding the basket and Tupperware, and hurried to Lenny's side. "Well?" she asked.

"I don't know," he answered.

"Her door's still closed," I offered.

"We should make sure she's okay," Sonia shared.

That snapped Lenny to action. "Yes, we should." He stood up and led the way to Beverly's office.

Just as he lifted his hand to knock, the door swung open from the inside, which made Beverly gasp in surprise and Lenny jump back in response.

"Sorry," Beverly and Lenny apologized in perfect unison.

"Oh, jeez Louise," Sonia said, shaking her head at the scene.

"We saw him leave," Lenny explained right away. "We just wanted to check on you."

"Of course," Beverly said. She ran her hands down the sides of her pants. "And I was coming out to talk to you. To all of you."

"Okay," Lenny said.

"About that lawyer," Beverly said unnecessarily.

"Yes?" Sonia couldn't help herself. "What was that all about?"

Lenny leaned in toward Beverly, his whole body on edge. I hugged my arms around my waist and looked toward the circ desk. No one was there, so we were okay for the moment. I looked back at Beverly. She kept running a finger over her locket, over the memory of her sister held safely inside.

"That was Alan Stutler. He's a lawyer for the Harriston family."

Harriston. How did I know that name?

"Mr. Stutler was here to discuss the final will and testament of Walter Harriston."

All the queasiness that had formed in my gut when Mr. Stutler presented his card disappeared the instant I heard Beverly say Walter. When I checked in his five movies on Tuesdays, I was always thrown for a quick second when the screen flashed the name *Walter*. To me, he was just Wally. And always would be.

"It appears"—and here Beverly cleared her throat and lowered her voice significantly—"it appears our dear Wally has left a great portion of his estate to the Foxfield Public Library." She motioned us closer to add, "And apparently, he had quite the estate."

Lenny's mouth fell open and his entire body slid against the doorframe, as if digesting this news and supporting his own weight were two things he could not possibly do at the same time. Sonia clapped her hand tightly over her open mouth. My eyes welled and before I knew it, a few happy tears spilled down my face.

"He left us money?" Sonia spoke through her fingers, still physically trapping her excitement in with one hand while holding her cookies with the other. "He left the library money?"

Beverly nodded. "Yes. He left us money. He left us a lot of money." Then she released her locket, crossed her arms in front of her torso, and lifted her chin in triumph. "Let's see them try to close our library now."

Wally

->>> · <<<-

The next week, Wally's endowment to the library was on the front page of the *Biweekly*. It covered the *entire* front page, and also got written up in the weekend Metro section of the regional newspaper. The phone at the library rang off the hook for days, and Beverly was more than happy this time around to talk to reporters. She said things like, "Clearly, the library is highly regarded by the public" and "Clearly, the library meets a very important need in the community."

Wally's endowment would cover the cost of all the building repairs, and there'd *still* be money left to establish a maintenance fund the library could pull from for years. It wasn't too expensive for the town to keep the library open anymore. Between the endowment, the petition, the appeals made by the well-connected Mrs. Evans, and all the press, Mayor Trippley abandoned his plans to shut us down. Operation Save Library was a success!

When Lenny arrived on the morning we heard the great news, he burst through the front door with a huge bouquet of flowers in his arms and sang, "Good morning to you, and a good morning it is!" He carried the bouquet to the circ desk and placed it right next to Wally's vase.

"These are from the Bean Pot owners. They loved the story in the paper about Wally's weekly flower, so they bought us these to honor his memory."

"They're not the only ones," Sonia said, and gestured around her.

There were flowers everywhere.

A bouquet of sunflowers from the Floral Parade sat on a table in the reading room, and an arrangement of dahlias and daisies from Barbara's Bouquet decorated the counter by the watercooler. A patron who was in the library the day of Wally's collapse had dropped off a vase stuffed with chrysanthemums and delphiniums, and another local family had sent a bouquet with a card saying *In memory of Walter.*

We also received a rainbow-colored bouquet of carnations in a frosted white vase with a card thanking us for being such an important part of Wally's life. It was from Kim Harriston and Walter Harriston Jr., Wally's kids.

So it turned out I didn't need to stop at the market to buy a flower for Wally's vase that morning, but I didn't know that until after I bought it. My single pink rose was seriously over-shadowed by all the large bouquets, but I refreshed the water and set the rose in its usual spot anyway, where Wally liked it. The desk wouldn't have looked right without it.

And pink was the obvious choice for this week's flower once I learned that pink stood for gratitude and appreciation. We would all be forever grateful to Wally—Beverly, Sonia, Lenny, me, Black Hat Guy, and all the other people who relied on the library to be here for them, whether they came in twice a day or twice a year.

It was 11:20 in the morning, August 29, and my last free Tuesday before school began. The library was bustling with people. Black Hat Guy—I mean Rusty—was in his quotes chair, wearing his purple AWO shirt, reading the newspaper before heading off to work at the shelter. The elderly Jansen couple were seated together in the reading room, leaning over the same magazine. A man wearing a tie and khakis was signing on to a computer next to a twentysomething-year-old research-ing online. Two moms in the children's room were chatting while choosing board books, and a woman in shorts and hiking boots was making copies at the Xerox machine while sipping an iced coffee in a to-go Bean Pot cup.

Beverly came out of her office, a pen and paper in her hand. She walked around the library to every flower arrangement and copied down the names of the senders. I knew she would be working on thank-you notes all morning. "It's never a burden to write them," she had told me. "If you have a lot of them to write, it's because you've been blessed."

Beverly answered a question for someone at the computer catalog, then nodded and smiled at the women in the children's room before heading back to her office.

"Beverly, wait." I rushed over to her. "I have an idea. For your thank-yous."

"I'd love to hear it," she said, her face relaxed and happy in a way it hadn't been for weeks.

"What if I made a small drawing of Wally's flower to include in all the letters? Like a little Wally souvenir?"

Beverly smiled wide. "I love that idea, Jamie. Wonderful." Then she asked, "Do you need paper?"

"No, I have my sketchbook with me. Always. So I'll cut paper out of there."

Beverly showed me the size of her stationery so I could match it, then returned to her office to write.

The library was full, but no one needed my help just then. I had finished all my shelving, and my shelf-reading work and the book drops could wait.

I grabbed my sketchbook, sharpened my pencil, and pulled a stool over to the circ counter. I looked closely at the pink rose. It was just a flower, but it seemed like more to me, the way it stood tall and strong, quiet but sure.

The petals reminded me of pages in a book, each one telling a small part of its story—the story of Wally and his weekly visits to the library, and the story of my summer in this place.

I put my pencil on the blank white page and started to sketch. I had a lot of drawings to make.

But this first sketch I drew, this one was going to be for me.

Beverly

>>>·<<<

The next morning when I walked into the library, Sonia and Lenny were at the circ desk, eating cookies and acting goofier than Vic on a sugar high after too many KitKat bars. They were also wearing matching shirts, which I was about to tease them for until I got a better look. The Library Friends League shirts!

"They're here!" I blurted out.

"Fresh from the printer," Lenny said happily. "We don't need the shirts to save the library anymore, Jamie. We need them to gloat that we won!"

"No, Lenny." Sonia elbowed him. "We are gracious victors. We wear these shirts in celebration of our new Friends League, which we definitely need, yes?"

"Of course, of course. I'm nothing if not a good winner,"

Lenny said, "even though the things I'd like to say to that Trippley—"

And Sonia cut him off by shoving an entire cookie into his mouth.

"Jamie, look. Lenny made a spine poem," Sonia said, pointing it out to me and wiping crumbs off Lenny's face at the same time. "We're leaving it on display all week."

It was just three titles:

The Public Library
Like Life
Reason for Hope

"It's perfect," I said.

"Even without any scat in it," Lenny added, laughing. Then he told me to go downstairs to grab a shirt.

The shirts were organized in the box by size and I helped myself to three of them, one for my mom, one for Aunt Julie, and one for me. I pulled mine on over the tank top I was wearing. It smelled slightly of ink and a lot like the cardboard box it had traveled in, but I didn't want to wait to wash it first. I wanted to match Sonia and Lenny, and I wanted to celebrate our victory.

I looked in the mirror over the staff kitchen sink. I loved the shirts, and not just because of who drew the logo. I loved them because of what they stood for—this place, this summer, this whole community coming together, all we had been through and how much it all mattered.

Every member of the Friends League would receive a shirt, and we'd sell the rest at our next fund-raising event. And we would have fund-raising events now. The Friends League would organize book sales, bake sales, T-shirt sales, all to benefit the library.

As I reached the top of the steps, I had a perfect view of Beverly in her office, the door wide open, yet another vase of flowers on her desk, dwarfing the computer monitor beside it. She looked up and smiled at my T-shirt, then looked down at her own, and nodded me over to join her.

"They look wonderful, don't they?" she asked, smoothing out the front of her shirt with her hands.

"Yes, they're perfect," I said, walking into her office. I had never seen Beverly in a regular, untailored T-shirt before. It made her look as young as a college kid.

"We're swimming in flowers!" I said, rubbing a soft rose petal between my fingertips.

"Yes, well." Beverly smiled. "Mrs. Evans sent these. Her note said she was always happy to help 'fight the good fight.'"

"That was nice of her," I said. "She did so much for us."

"She did. And the funny thing is, I sent her a bouquet just

like this one last night. From the same florist even. She should get it today. I wanted to thank her personally for all her help. It might be the same *exact* bouquet," she said again in disbelief. "That's a bit awkward, isn't it?"

I smiled wide, thinking back to my very first day in the library, the very first time I met Beverly. I couldn't help saying, "Well, what's so bad about awkward?"

Beverly let out a sigh. "Nothing, I guess."

"Anyway, they say great minds think alike," I offered.

"Speaking of great minds"—Beverly looked at me almost sheepishly—"the Friends League thinks we should have a Teen Advisory Committee. They'd like regular input to make sure we're providing all the services teens need, and they also want to increase the number of teenagers in town who use the library. We may have won our fight with Trippley today, but the budget issue will likely resurface in the future. Having even more of the community on our side will help us next time around."

She continued, "Several people have suggested that you"—and she emphasized that last word—"be the head of this teen committee. And I agree that you are fully suited for the job. It would be an official position with some responsibilities, but could be flexible around your school commitments." She clasped her hands in front of her and rubbed them together. "So"—she smiled then, really big—"I'm not even going to ask you what you think. I just want you to tell me you'll do it."

I felt something open up and bloom inside me. I wasn't that kid who messed up anymore. I was that responsible, trustworthy, helpful kid who worked at the library. I was that kid people thought could be a leader. And Beverly agreed. Tingles ran through my whole body, and I didn't even have to think about it.

"Yes, I'll do it!"

Beverly came around the back of her desk and put her arms around me. Her hug felt just right, like a book sliding perfectly into place on its shelf. Before she let me go, she whispered in my ear, "Good for you, Jamie. Well done."

And in that moment I had to admit that I really *had* done well for myself. From middle school scandal queen assigned to community service to being lauded in the local newspaper to becoming head of the Teen Advisory Committee, all in just a few months. Without meaning to, and without expecting it at all, I had managed to have the best summer of my life.

"Well, I have a million and one calls to make now. How about you go get to it at the circ desk? I'd like to wring as much work out of you as possible these last few days." She winked at me, but it looked a little more like a flinch than a wink. It was awkward, but it was Beverly.

"Sure thing," I told her, and I got back to work.

Trina

-»»·«««-

Everyone in town seemed to come to the library that day. We were busier than ever. I was trying to work quickly every time books were returned to get them double-checked and placed right away on the shelving cart. We had a lot less counter space than usual because of the flowers everywhere.

A mom came in with her two daughters, and each little girl handed over a flower they had picked for Wally. They were buttercups, that tiny yellow flower that grew like a weed and cast a faint yellow reflection on your skin when you held it under your chin. When Vic and I were in kindergarten, she taught me that if you could see the yellow it meant you liked butter, and if you couldn't see it, it meant you didn't. It was silly, but we still tested each other every time we found one outside.

"Where is Wally's flower vase?" the older girl asked, her voice quiet and practiced.

I pointed her to the side of the circ desk where Wally's pink rose stood. I lowered the jar down to her height and she dropped her buttercup in. Then her sister did the same with hers. The younger one covered her mouth with her hands and giggled at the sight of her small flower next to the rose, while the older one smiled a smile that showed every tooth in her mouth. I put the vase back in its spot and thanked the girls. The mom thanked me in return and they left. I watched as they skipped together down the path, hopping and spinning in the afternoon sun as they went.

When a lull finally arrived around four o'clock in the afternoon, Lenny and Sonia took a minute to retreat to the staff kitchen together for a coffee and cookie break. They were discussing which restaurant to try on their date tonight, and when I heard Lenny suggest Jade Noodle Shop, I knew they were going to have a perfect night together.

I had just finished double-checking a stack of DVDs when the door jingled itself open again and three people entered.

Trina and her two shadows.

I swallowed to get the lump out of my throat, but then realized there wasn't any lump there. I was actually fine.

"Ahhh, air-conditioning," Izzy said the moment she stepped inside.

Trina walked right up to the desk, with Izzy and Amanda

behind her. She dropped an art book on the counter, not even bothering to put it in the returns bin. I watched her eyes scan my hair and then jump to my shirt. She did an eye roll/head shake combination, as if my very existence was infringing on her human rights.

Then Izzy noticed my shirt. "Oh my God, that's the design you were talking about!" Her voice was loud and excited.

"I wasn't talking about it." Trina immediately dismissed any hint of enthusiasm she might have shown about the Friends League.

Izzy's face dropped into a pout. I almost felt sorry for her.

"Well your mom *did* show us that drawing at your house," Izzy carefully defended herself.

"Whatever," Trina muttered.

"Did you get yours yet?" Amanda asked Trina, then turned to me and said, "Are they for sale?"

Trina answered, "Why would I wear that?" at the same moment that I answered, "Yes, we're doing a fund-raiser."

Trina half glared at me, but when I looked her right back in the eye without a flinch or a blush or a blink, she rolled her eyes again, lazily, and looked away.

"I like it," Amanda said then. "It's a pretty cool shirt."

Trina turned to her, a challenge on her face.

"For a library," Amanda added, a little less confidently.

"Whatever," Trina said again, apparently running out of vocabulary.

The library bells jingled and an older woman with snow-white hair walked in. She carefully slid two books into the returns bin and then said, "Good afternoon."

"Good afternoon," I repeated.

Trina and Izzy and Amanda just stood there and watched.

"Oh heavens, what a lovely top you're wearing," the woman exclaimed. "Isn't that marvelous!"

"Yes, thank you. They just came in," I responded, looking down at it. There was no doubt there was a tinge of pink on my cheeks when I looked at the shirt. The shirt was Trey, and I still liked Trey, and there was no way Trina didn't notice my blush.

But before she could say anything snarky or mean, the white-haired woman spoke. "I'll be back in a bit. I'm headed to the Large Print."

"Of course, just behind that wall," I directed her.

"Thank goodness for large print and the angel who invented it," she said, laughing to herself.

"We just got some brand-new mysteries in. They're on the top shelf," I added as she walked away. She waved a thank-you.

"C'mon," Trina snapped at her friends. "Let's get our cookbooks already." She marched around the circ desk to the room where the cookbooks were, and Izzy and Amanda followed in a line like obedient baby ducklings, just not nearly as cute.

The clock above the door said it was 4:31 in the afternoon. I glanced over at Black Hat Guy's chair. It was empty, but I wasn't surprised. I knew he was busy at the AWO, working with the dogs, learning from the staff, hopefully turning his volunteer gig into a paying job.

My eyes were drawn to the Alice quote on his chair again. *It's no use going back to yesterday, because I was a different person then.* My mind raced back to that Monday in June when I'd first stepped into the library to start my punishment. That was *many* yesterdays ago, and I was certainly as different a person then as Alice was before she fell down that rabbit hole. And yet, yesterday was still part of me. All my yesterdays were my history, my story, and even though I'd turned the page, those yesterdays' stories were still there. I was composed of every single yesterday of my life, and they all added up to right now. And every single day I woke up with the opportunity to be something, some*one*, new.

"I'm so hungry now," Izzy complained to Trina and Amanda as they emerged from the back room, "from all those photos. I need FOOD!"

"Let's go buy chips at the pharmacy," Amanda suggested.

"Yes, I need chips!" Izzy replied.

"We're getting these," Trina announced as she dropped a heavy stack of cookbooks on the counter before me.

"That was quick," I said.

"I know what I'm doing," Trina assured me. "I'm having another party, an end-of-summer bash, and I know exactly what to make." She flung her library card on top of the books instead of handing it to me.

Sonia always said there were two kinds of people, and that was the kind Trina was: a card-dropper.

Trina was never going to forgive me for my Korea exhibit in second grade or for my yearbook victory in fifth. She was never going to give me a chance, like a book you had once judged by its cover and rejected, but later were willing to give a fair try.

Trina was never going to give me a fair try.

And as I thought about that, two words suddenly floated into my head, carrying with them a special power. So I said them out loud. "Duck feathers."

"What?" Trina asked, looking at me like I had finally revealed my true insanity for the world to see.

"Let it roll off your back," I kept going, hearing my mom's brave voice in my own.

"What are you talking about?" She scrunched her whole face up at me in total confusion.

"Nothing," I said, and felt a smile break across my face so

wide and so strong that I couldn't hide it and I couldn't fight it.

I scanned her card and books and handed them all back to her. "Have a nice day," I said.

Trina took her pile and looked at me. "Uh-huh," was her reply.

And then she left. Izzy followed her out, talking about chips, but Amanda turned back and returned to the desk, to me.

"You know, Trey's outside right now and he might want to see that shirt," she said. "Mrs. Evans said he spent *forever* drawing it."

My eyes jumped automatically to the window in the front door to look for him.

Amanda shrugged and added, "Just sayin'." Then she ran outside and caught up with her friends.

My stomach did a quick jumping jack and my heart did some kind of flitter beat I had never felt before.

Trey was outside.

I left the circ desk and ran downstairs to grab a shirt for him.

I looked down at the design on the shirt, the swirls of black vine dipping and climbing, the swoopy calligraphy both delicate and strong at the same time. Then I peered through the window and saw Trey seated outside, just as Amanda had said, his sketchbook in his lap, his hand moving over the paper in slow, measured strokes.

Sonia came back upstairs with her coffee. It was in a mug that said *Professional Bookworm*.

"Very cute." I gestured to her mug.

"Yes. Online. You can find anything," she said. "I ordered paintbrush cookie cutters, too. They should come this week. Don't tell Lenny, though. It's a surprise."

"Okay," I assured her, "I won't."

Sonia took a sip of coffee and placed her mug in its usual spot, right above the money drawer.

"I'm going outside for a minute, Sonia," I told her.

Sonia grinned knowingly at me. "Of course you are, mami. You go. I've got the desk."

I pushed through the main door, walked under the musical bells, and started toward Trey. He was sitting at the far end of the path in a patch of sun, focused and still. I walked slowly, enjoying the heat on my back, the birdsong playing in the blue blanket of sky above me. My stomach was doing flips, but they were smaller than usual. I almost liked the way they felt.

I walked toward Trey because I finally knew how to deal.

I walked toward Trey because it was time to play the cards I had, and the cards I had all said the same thing: Know yourself. Be yourself.

And I was ready to do that.

I stepped closer and held the T-shirt out in front of me like both an invitation and a thank-you.

"Trey," I called, my voice crisp and sure.

He turned toward me, his hand raised to his forehead, squinting against the sun. Then the corners of his mouth moved, lifted up into a smile, and the beauty mark by his left eye gleamed in the strong shine of light. He let his pencil drop to his lap.

"Jamie," he said. "Hi."

Principal Shupe

Foxfield Middle School

September 5

What I Learned from My Community Service Assignment

1. Libraries are more than just books.

2. You can know the players and know yourself and still make a mistake.

3. Freshly brewed coffee smells amazing.

4. What looks like a bird's nest is not always a bird's nest.

5. Sometimes a mistake is the best thing that can happen to you.

6. Never judge a muffin by its ingredients.

7. Everyone has a story.

8. It's important to know when to turn the page.

9. Community service doesn't feel like a punishment when you work with incredible people.

10. The quote hidden on the back of Rusty Shine's chair reads: I have always imagined that Paradise will be a kind of library. I learned that I completely agree.

Sincerely,

Jamie Bunn

Quotes from
BLACK HAT GUY'S CHAIR

To be or not to be.

—*William Shakespeare*

Call me Ishmael.

—*Herman Melville*

Quoth the raven "Nevermore."

—*Edgar Allan Poe*

Tread softly because you tread on my dreams.

—*W. B. Yeats*

What is essential is invisible to the eye.

—*Antoine de Saint-Exupéry*

Time changes everything except something within us
which is always surprised by change.

—*Thomas Hardy*

Not all those who wander are lost.

—*J. R. R. Tolkien*

I have been bent and broken, but—I hope—
into a better shape.
—*Charles Dickens*

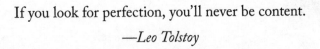

If you look for perfection, you'll never be content.
—*Leo Tolstoy*

To err is human, to forgive, divine.
—*Alexander Pope*

Wait for the common sense of the morning.
—*H. G. Wells*

It's no use going back to yesterday, because I was a
different person then.
—*Lewis Carroll*

I have always imagined that paradise will be a
kind of library.
—*Jorge Luis Borges*

Acknowledgments

I am grateful to so many people for bringing this book to life.

I cannot thank my agent, Joan Rosen, enough for all the good squidgy she has brought me. Thank you for the constant support, the marathon phone calls, the shopping tips, the publishing industry tutorials, and the surprise care packages of dark chocolate. You have been my greatest advocate and I'm so happy we found each other.

Thank you to my wonderful and talented team at HarperCollins for taking such good care of me and my work: Bethany Reis, Liz Byer, Shona McCarthy, Valerie Shea, Rosanne Lauer, Katie Fitch, Catherine San Juan, Erin Wallace, Vaishali Nayak, and Jacquelynn Burke. I am truly honored to work with editors Rosemary Brosnan, Karen Chaplin, and Jessica MacLeish. Jess, working with you on this book has been a gift. Thank you for your patience, insight, professionalism, and sensitivity. You shaped this book into a much better version of itself and taught me so much along the way.

Thank you to Chloe Bristol for her beautiful cover art. I still love looking at it.

I come from a family of readers and take comfort in knowing my parents and sisters and I will always share this common thread.

Thank you, Mom, for introducing me to the library as a little girl, for signing me up for the summer reading programs, and for driving me back to the library each time I finished a book so I could put another sticker on my chart.

Thank you, Dad, for always keeping a tally and proudly reporting how many books you read during your summer stays in New Hampshire.

Thank you to my sisters for embracing my book-nerdiness and gracefully allowing me to spew about books and authors even when you maybe didn't really want to listen.

My deepest and most heartfelt thanks go to Mike, Nina, and Jeffrey, who jumped on this rollercoaster with me and hung on tight. I could not have done this without you. Your generosity, compassion, and love inspired me and pulled me through. I love you more than anything.

And, of course, thank you to all the librarians and library lovers out there. This book is my celebration of you.